Even Fairies Bake Mistakes

DISCOVER DG GRAPHICS

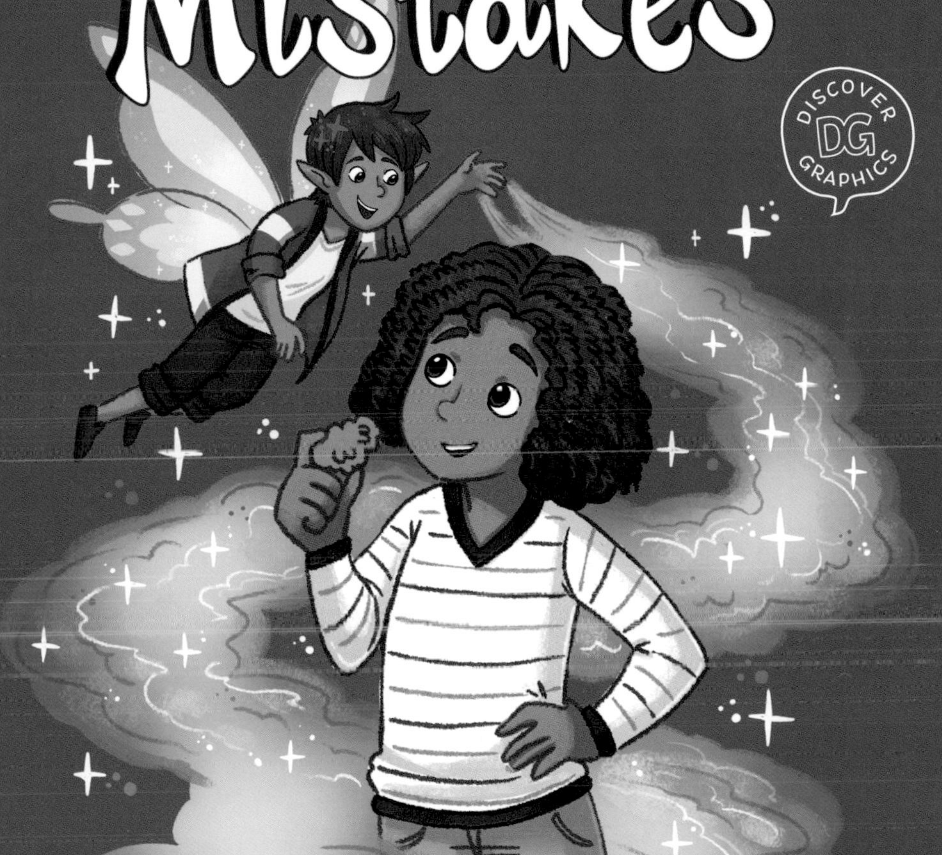

WRITTEN BY ELIZABETH PAG
ILLUSTRATED BY MICHELLE

PICTURE WINDOW BOO
a capstone imprint

Discover Graphics is published by Picture Window Books,
an imprint of Capstone.
1710 Roe Crest Drive
North Mankato, Minnesota 56003
www.capstonepub.com

Library of Congress Cataloging-in-Publication Data
Names: Pagel-Hogan, Elizabeth, author. | Simpson, Michelle, illustrator.
Title: Even fairies bake mistakes / by Elizabeth Pagel-Hogan ; illustrated by Michelle Simpson.
Description: North Mankato, Minnesota : Picture Window Books, a Capstone imprint, [2021] | Series: Discover graphics. Mythical creatures | Audience: Ages 5–7. | Audience: Grades K–1.
Identifiers: LCCN 2020031420 (print) | LCCN 2020031421 (ebook) | ISBN 9781515882022 (hardcover) | ISBN 9781515883074 (paperback) | ISBN 9781515891925 (eBook PDF) | ISBN 9781515892557 (kindle edition)
Subjects: LCSH: Graphic novels. | CYAC: Graphic novels. | Fairies—Fiction. | Baking—Fiction. | Errors—Fiction. | Perfectionism (Personality trait)—Fiction. | Contests—Fiction.
Classification: LCC PZ7.7.P13 Ev 2021 (print) | LCC PZ7.7.P13 (ebook) | DDC 741.5/973—dc23
LC record available at https://lccn.loc.gov/2020031420
LC ebook record available at https://lccn.loc.gov/2020031421

Summary: Dill is a fairy. He loves to bake. His flavors are fabulous. But there's one problem—his desserts look like a disaster! Can Dill's new friend, Ada, help him fix his mistakes and win the Fairyland Baking Contest?

Editorial Credits:
Editor: Mari Bolte; Designer: Kay Fraser; Media Researcher: Tracy Cummins; Production Specialist: Katy LaVigne

WORDS TO KNOW

confection—a sweet treat

ingredients—the different things that go into a mixture

recipe—the directions for making and cooking food

Printed and bound in the USA.

CAST OF CHARACTERS

Ada is a human girl who loves to help people. She also loves yummy treats!

Dill is a fairy who loves baking. He dreams of entering the Fairyland Baking Contest.

The other **Fairyland bakers** want to win the baking contest too.

The **Fairyland Baking Contest judges** will taste and decide whose baked goods are the best!

HOW TO READ A GRAPHIC NOVEL

Graphic novels are easy to read. Boxes called panels show you how to follow the story. Look at the panels from left to right and top to bottom.

Read the word boxes and word balloons from left to right as well. Don't forget the sound and action words in the pictures.

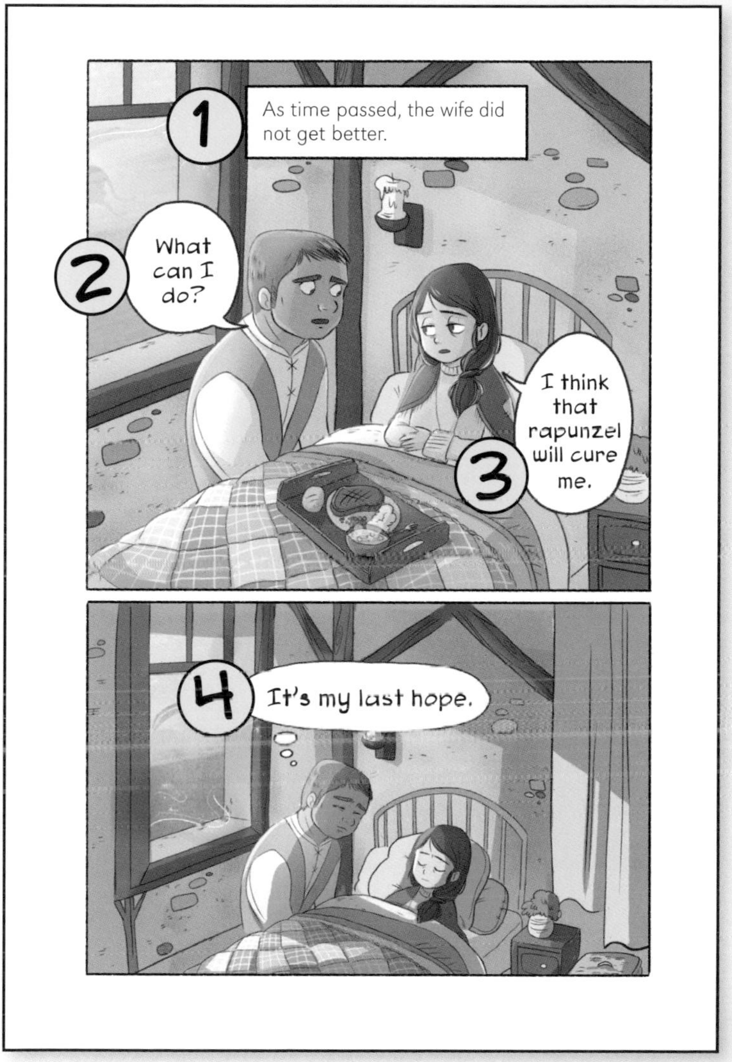
1
As time passed, the wife did not get better.
2
What can I do?
3
I think that rapunzel will cure me.
4
It's my last hope.

The pictures and the words work together to tell the whole story.

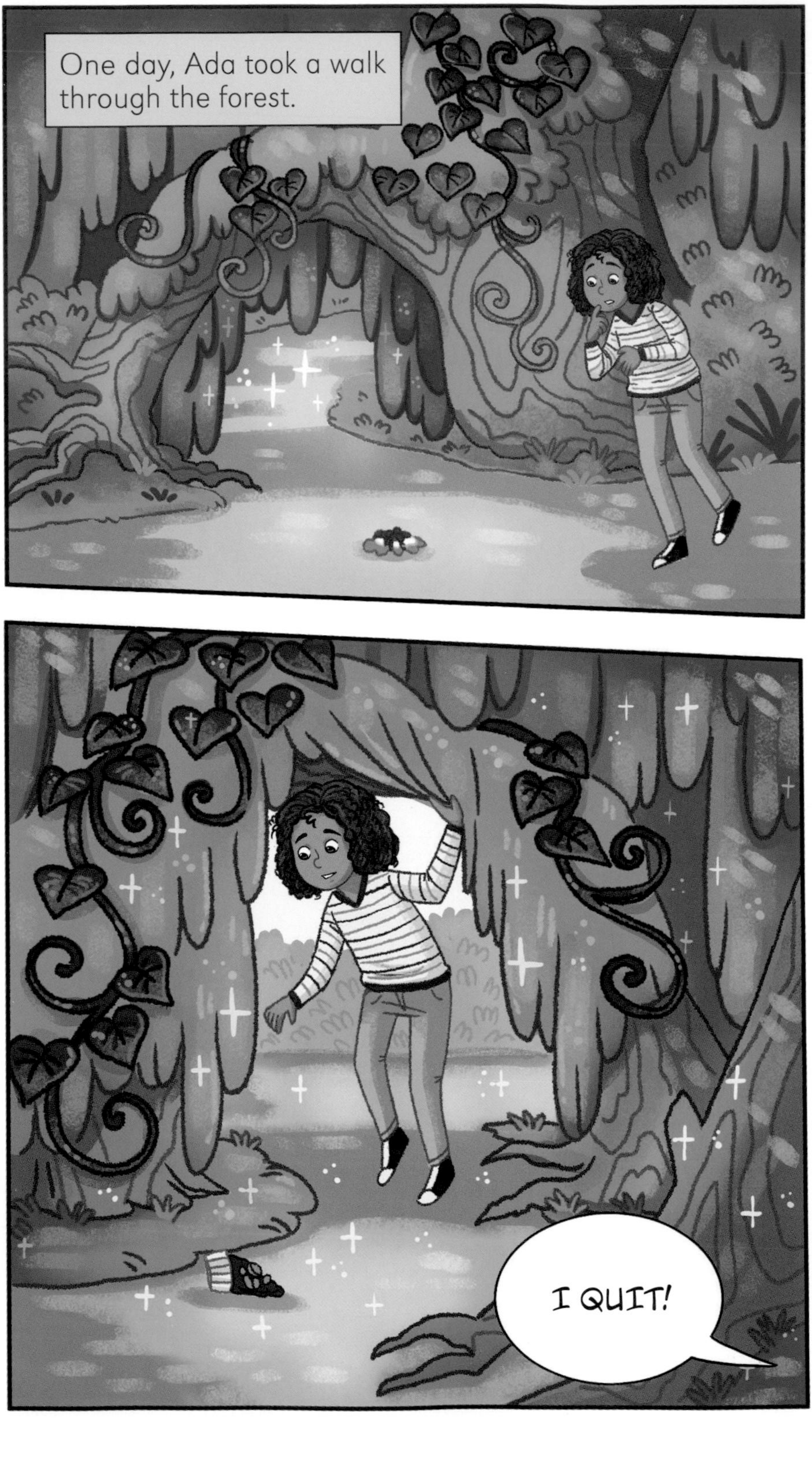
One day, Ada took a walk through the forest.
I QUIT!

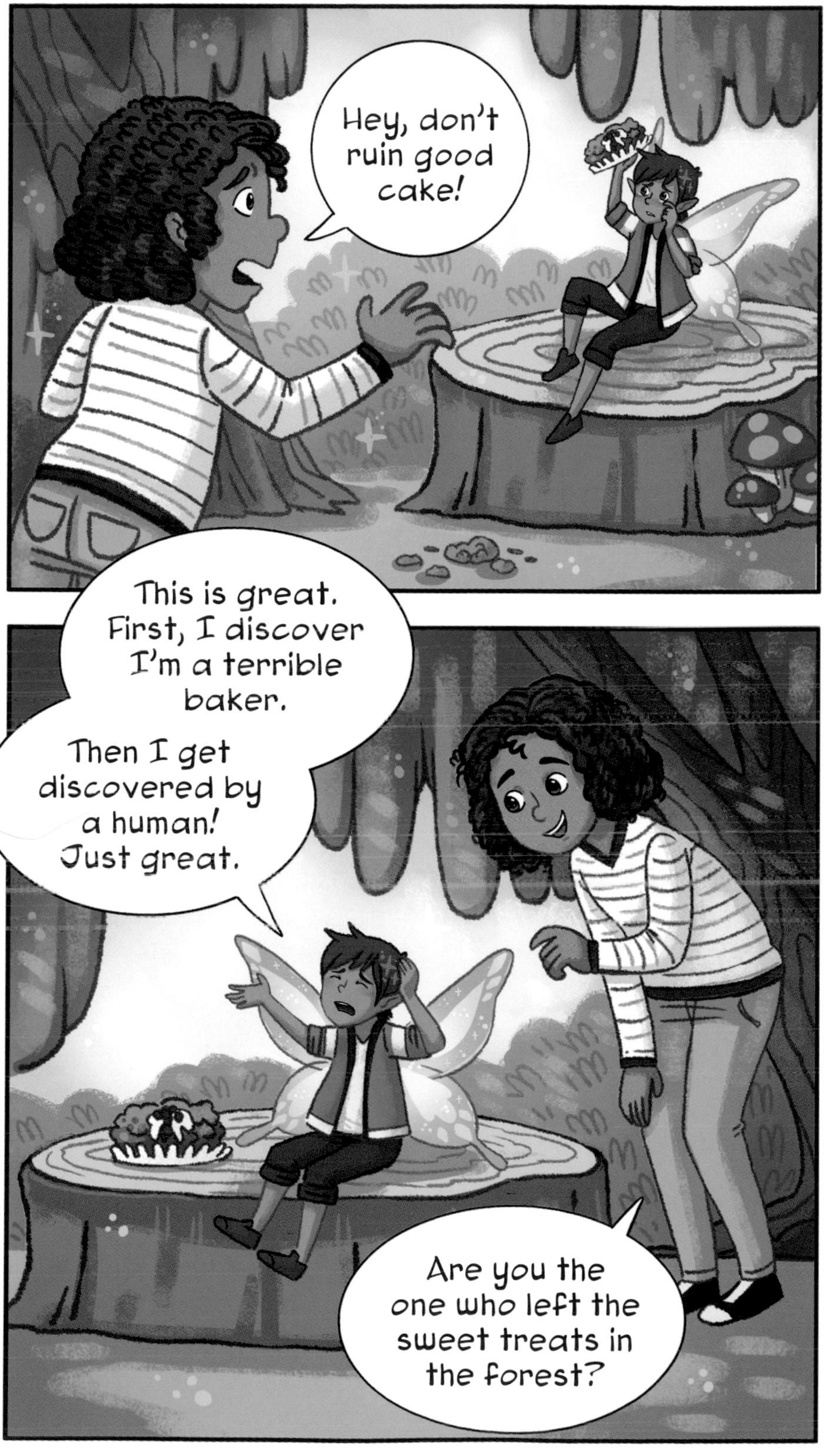

Hey, don't ruin good cake!
This is great. First, I discover I'm a terrible baker.
Then I get discovered by a human! Just great.
Are you the one who left the sweet treats in the forest?

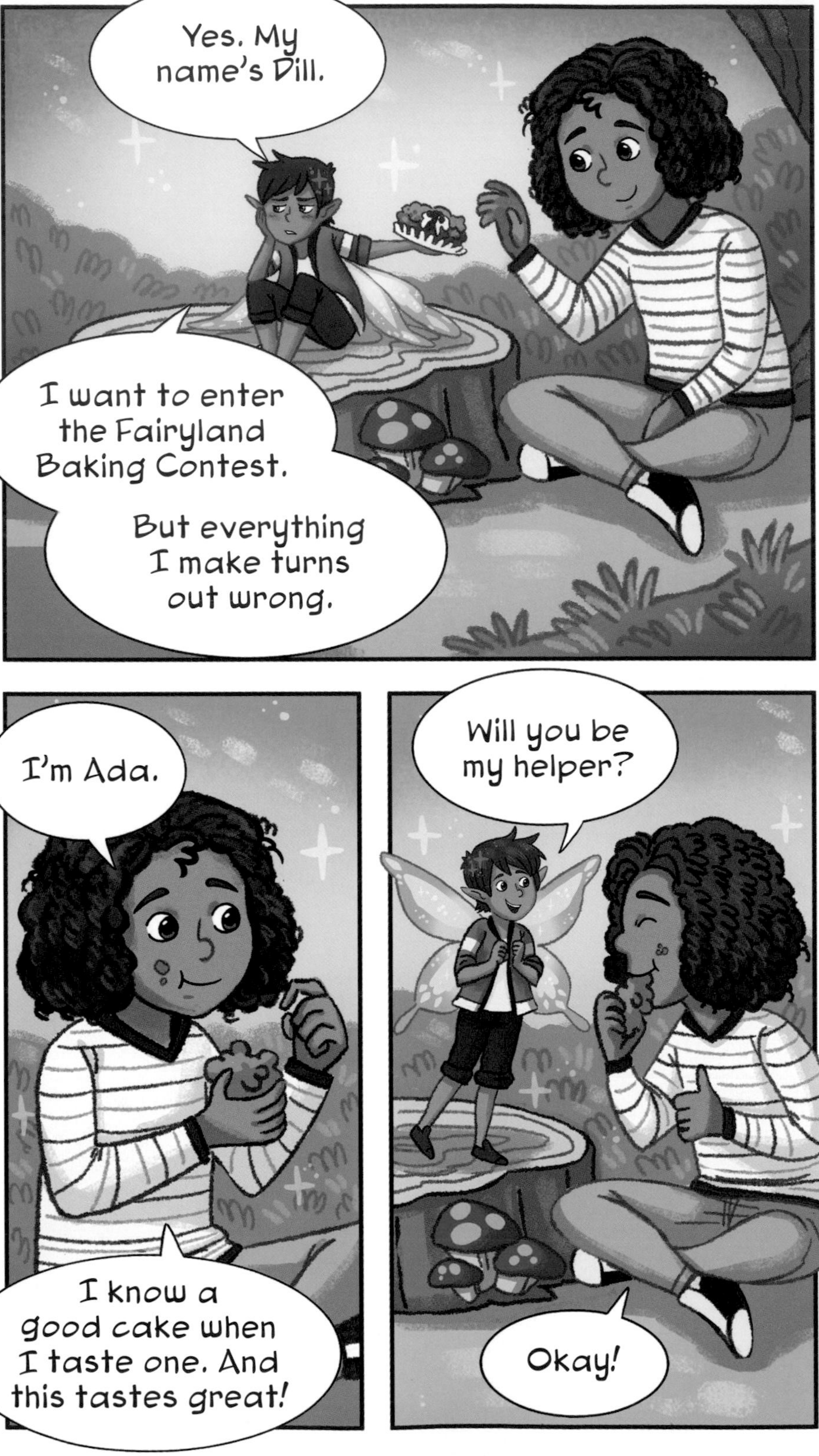
Yes. My name's Dill.
I want to enter the Fairyland Baking Contest.
But everything I make turns out wrong.
I'm Ada.
I know a good cake when I taste one. And this tastes great!
Will you be my helper?
Okay!

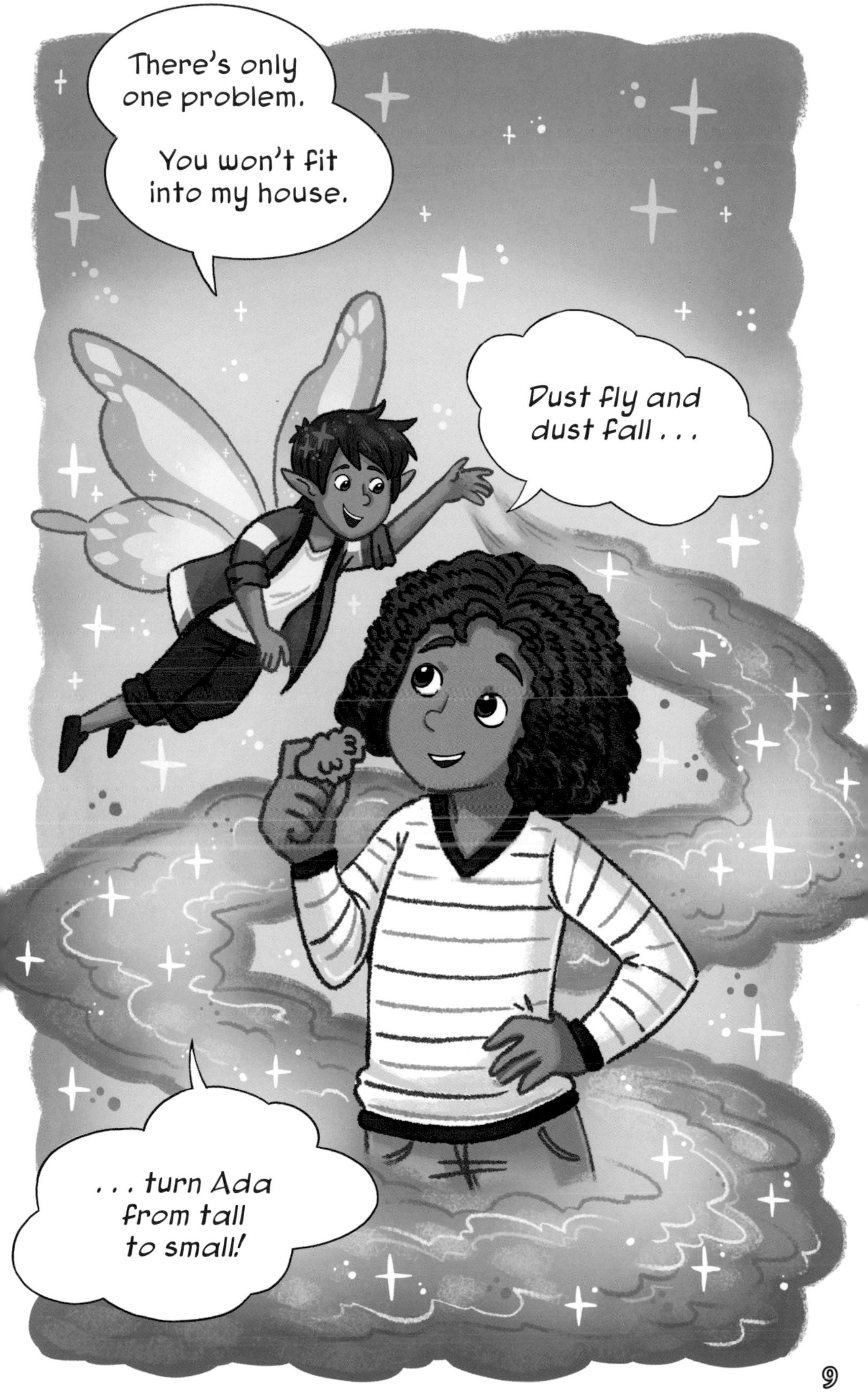
There's only one problem.
You won't fit into my house.
Dust fly and dust fall . . .
. . . turn Ada from tall to small!

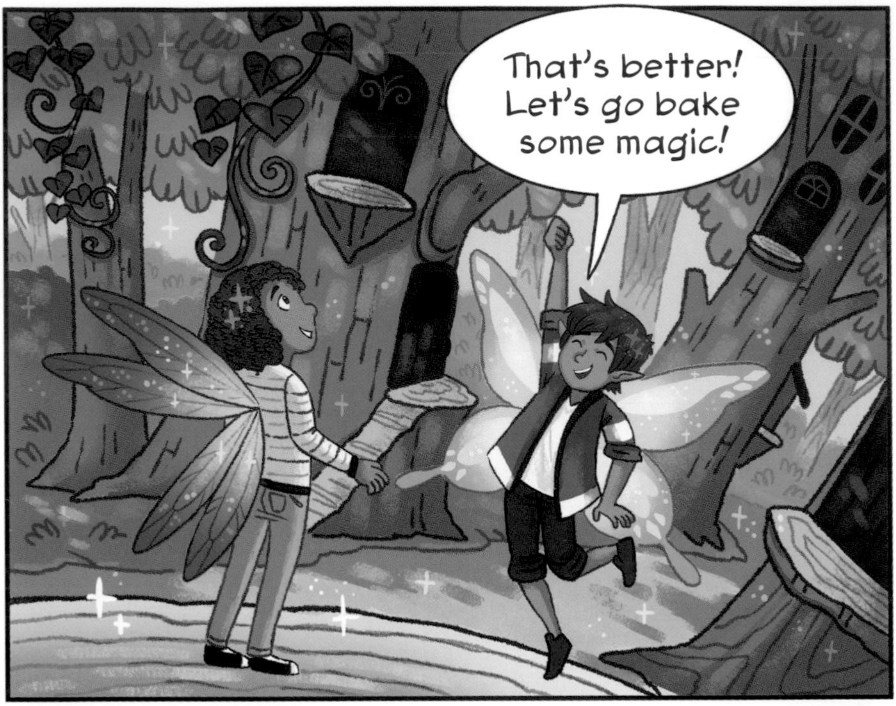
That's better! Let's go bake some magic!

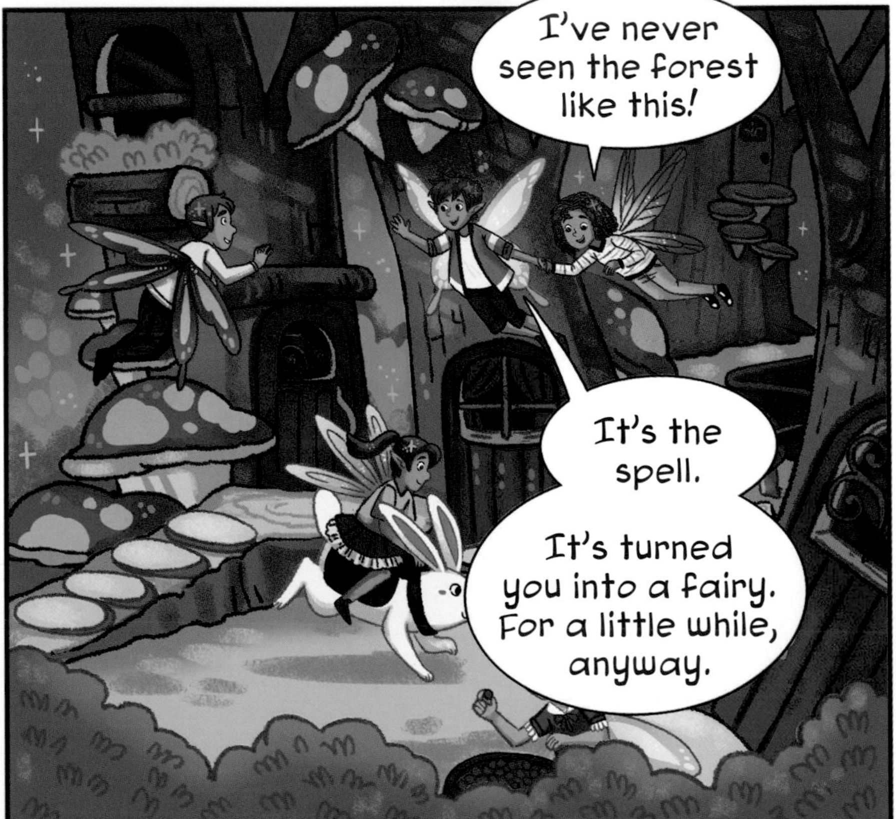
I've never seen the forest like this!
It's the spell.
It's turned you into a fairy. For a little while, anyway.

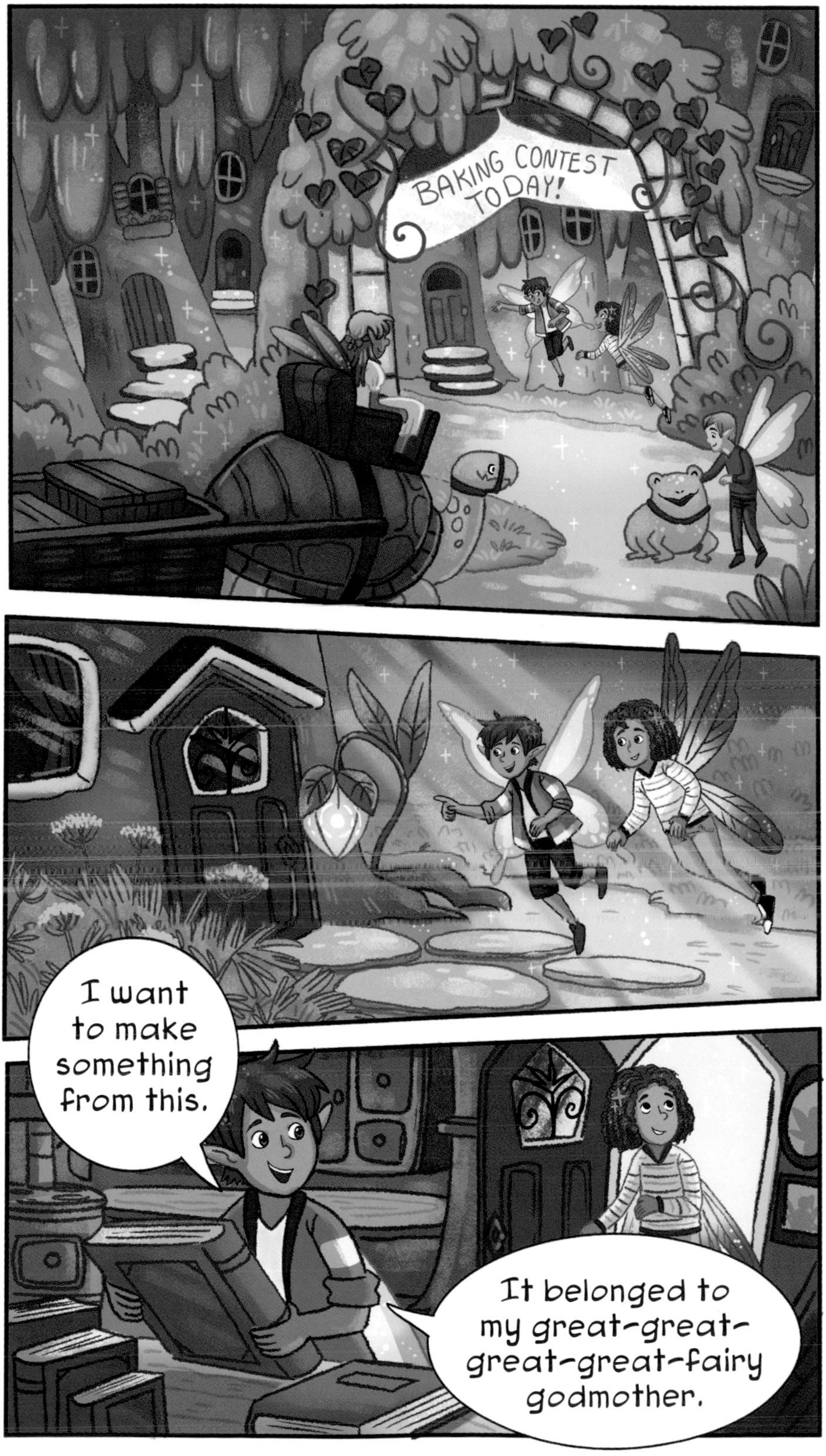
BAKING CONTEST TODAY!
I want to make something from this.
It belonged to my great-great-great-great-fairy godmother.

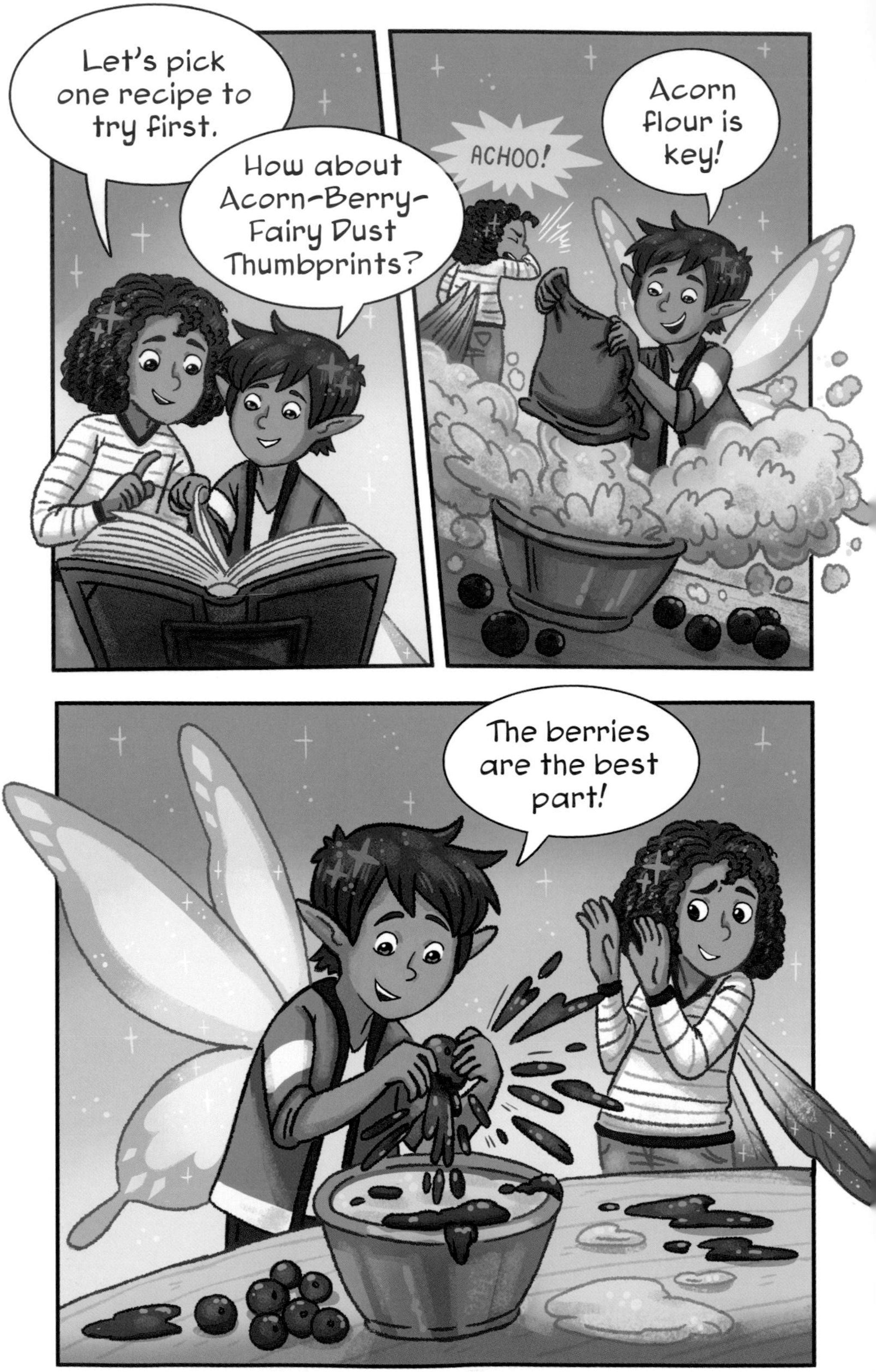
Let's pick one recipe to try first.
How about Acorn-Berry-Fairy Dust Thumbprints?
ACHOO!
Acorn flour is key!
The berries are the best part!

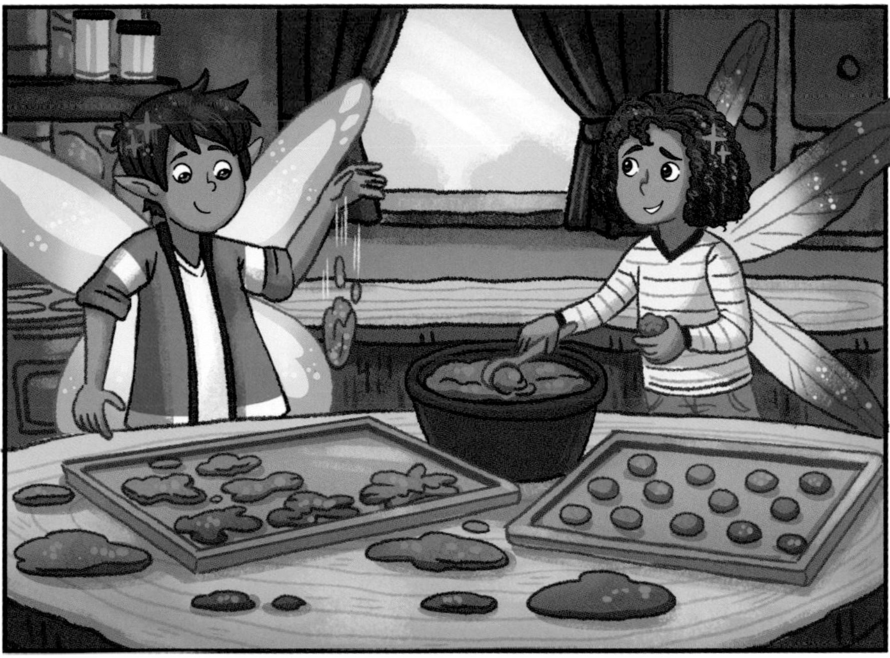

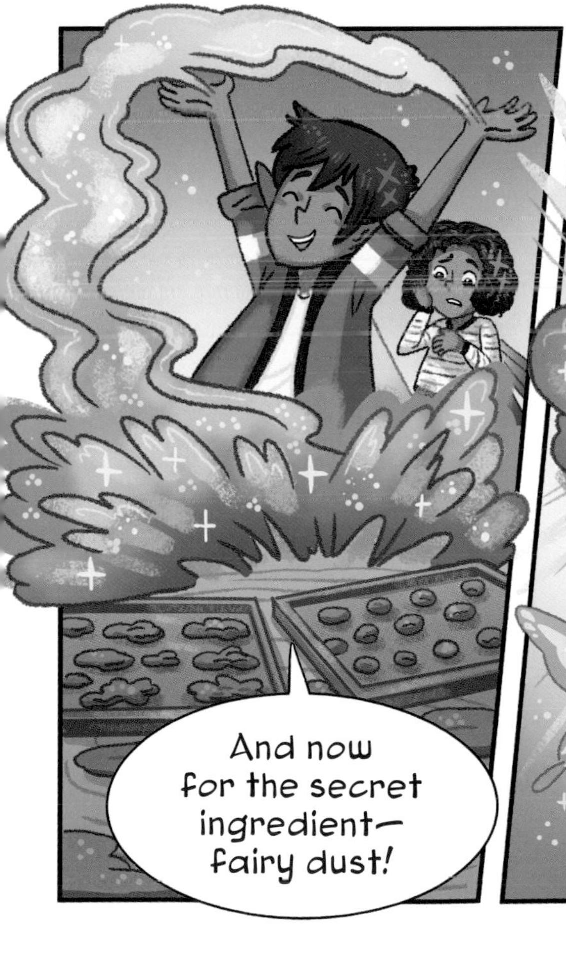
And now
for the secret
ingredient—
fairy dust!

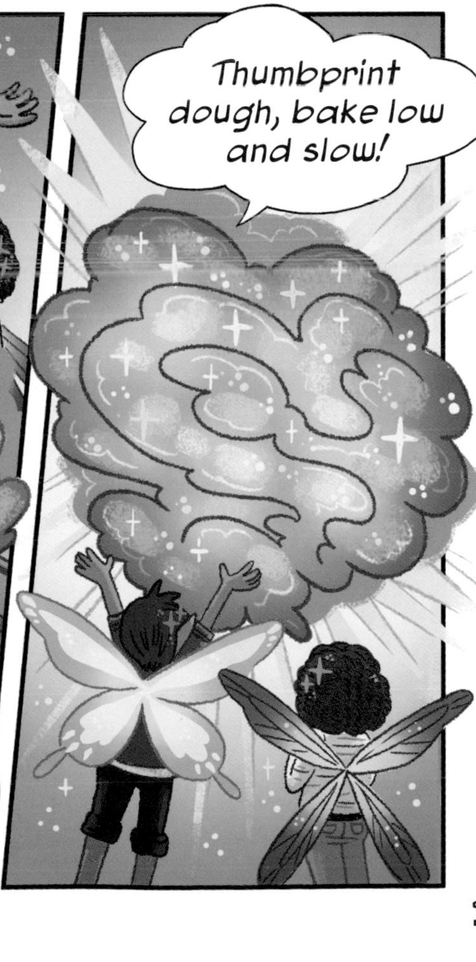
Thumbprint
dough, bake low
and slow!

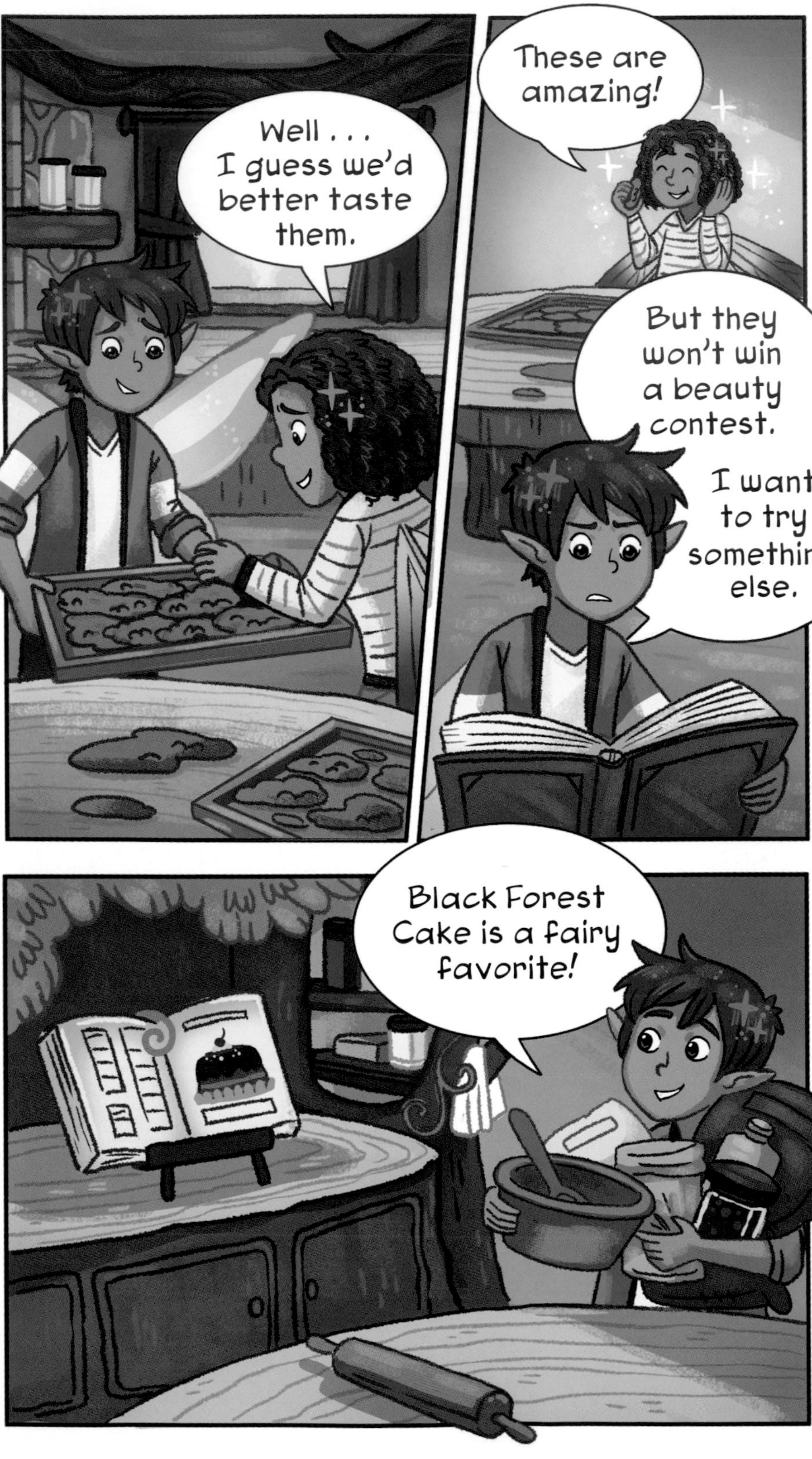
Well . . .
I guess we'd better taste them.
These are amazing!
But they won't win a beauty contest.
I want to try something else.
Black Forest Cake is a fairy favorite!

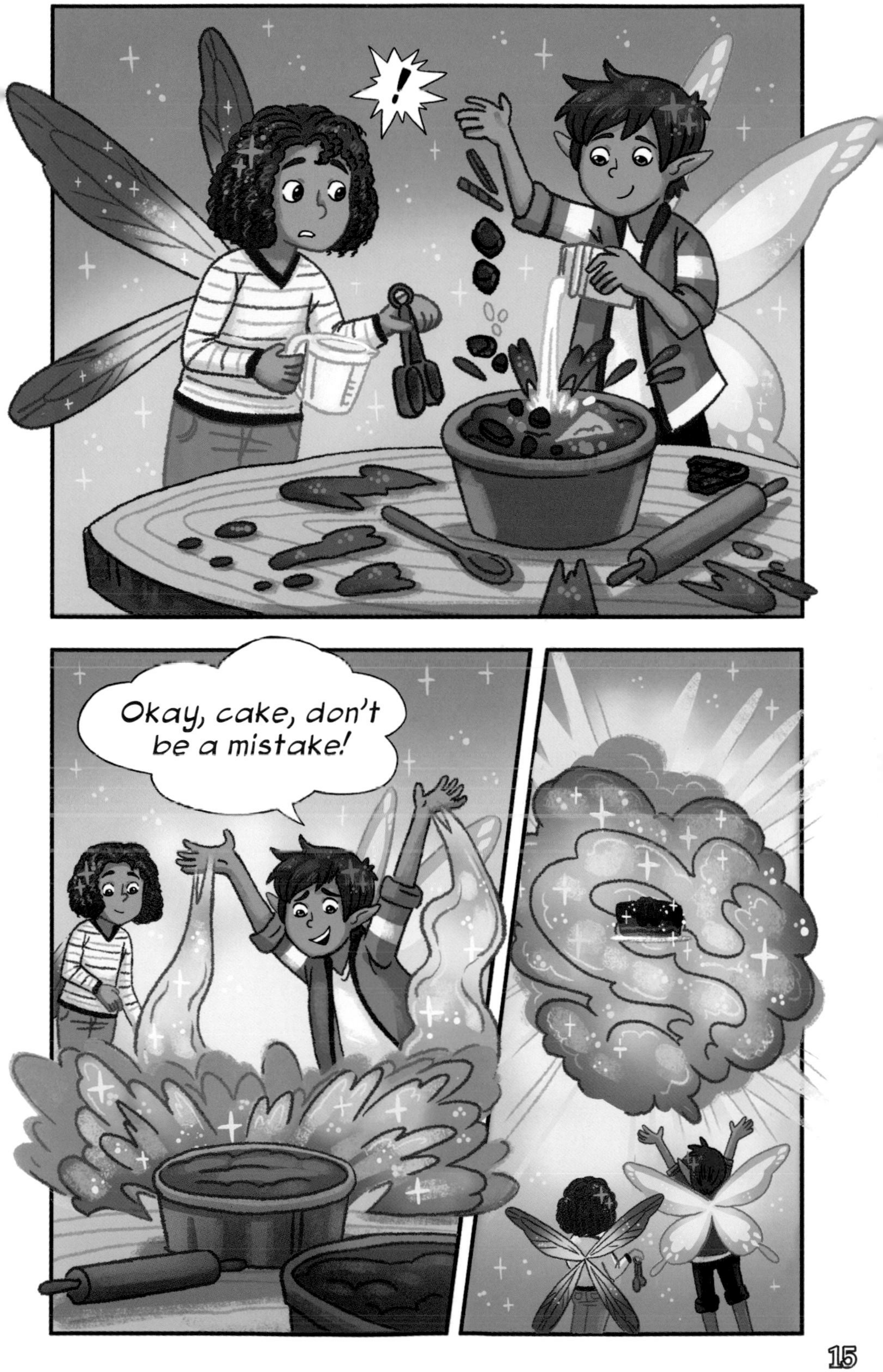
!
Okay, cake, don't be a mistake!

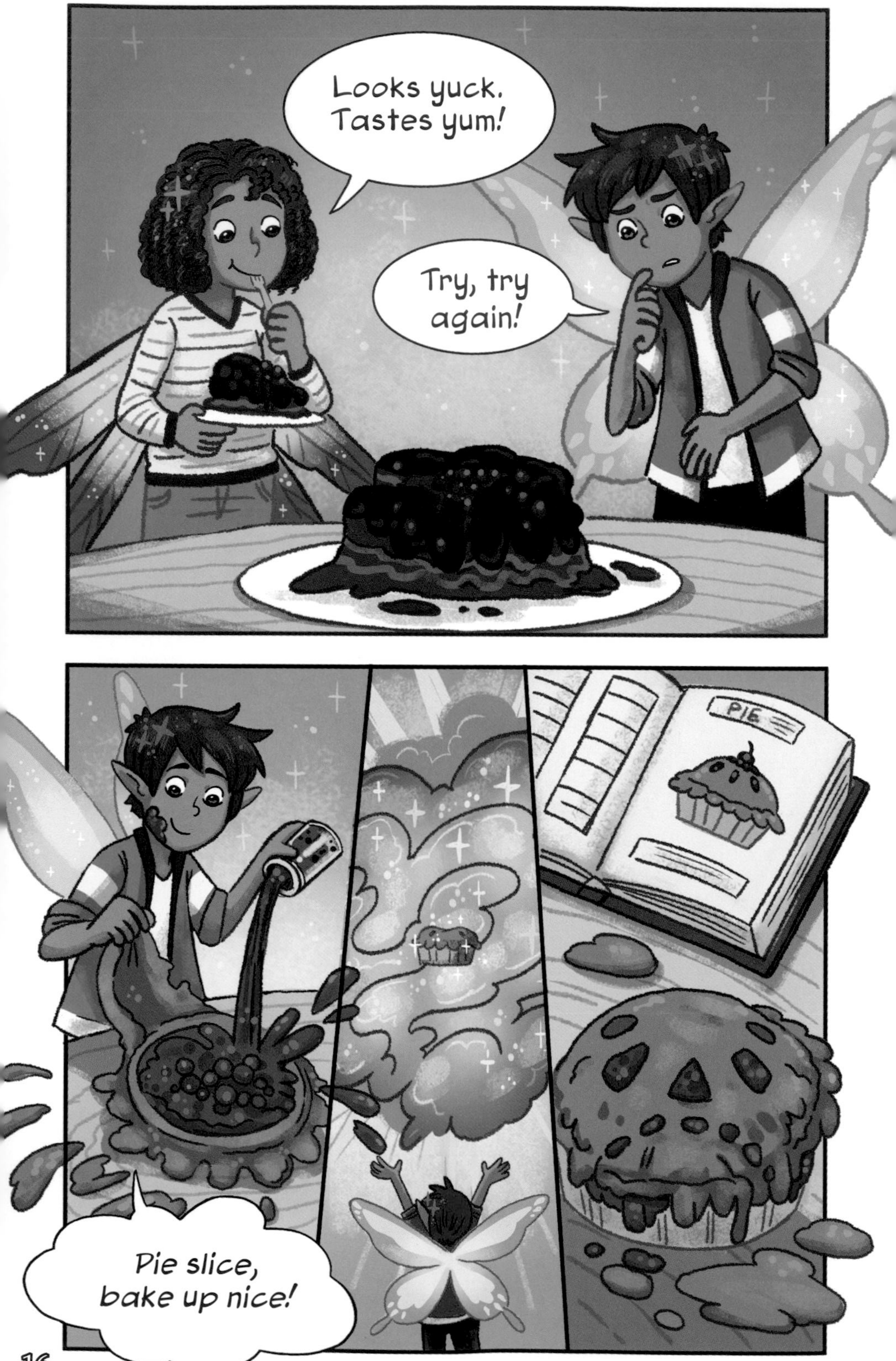
Looks yuck.
Tastes yum!
Try, try
again!
PIE
Pie slice,
bake up nice!

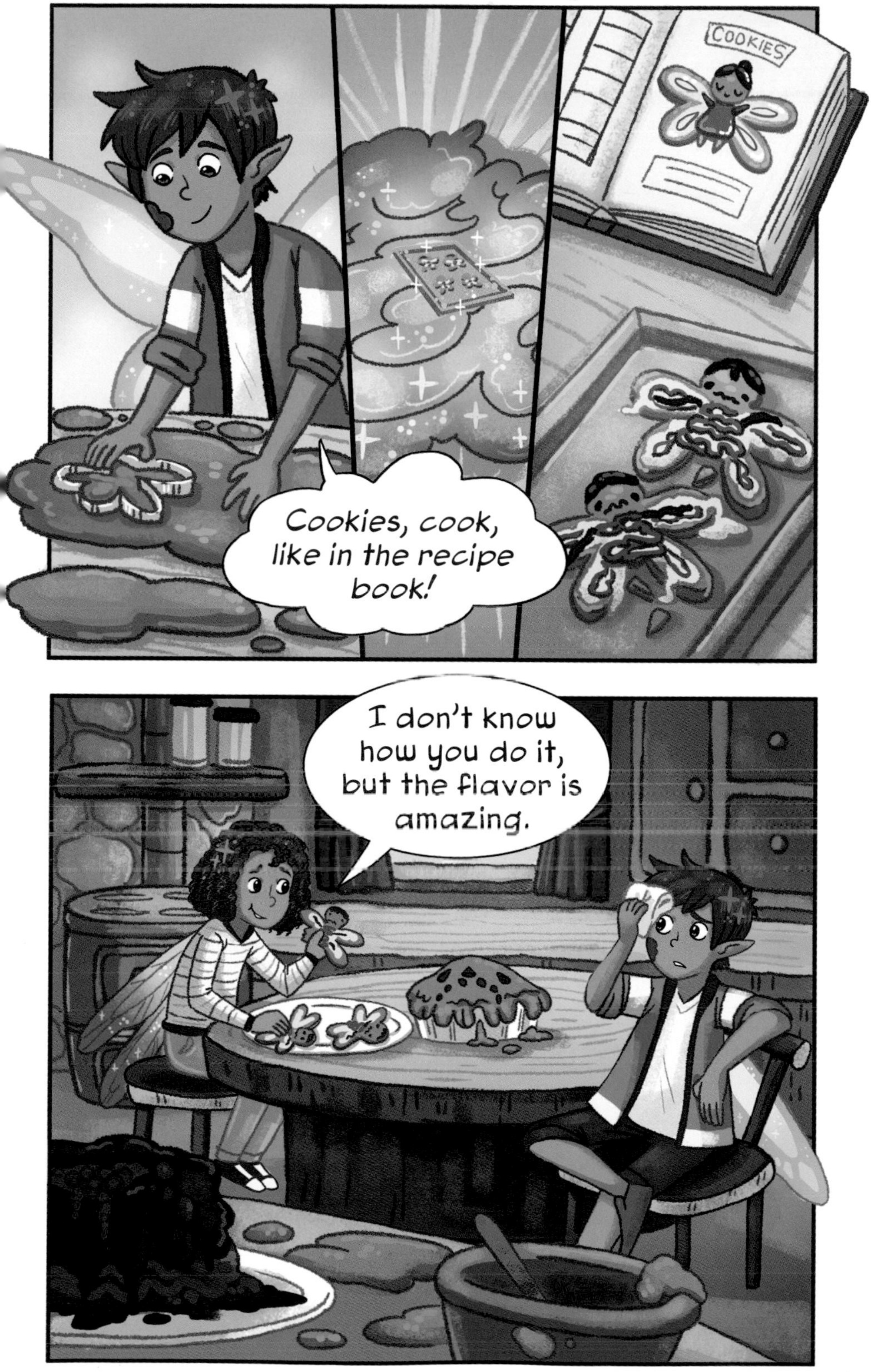
COOKIES
Cookies, cook, like in the recipe book!
I don't know how you do it, but the flavor is amazing.

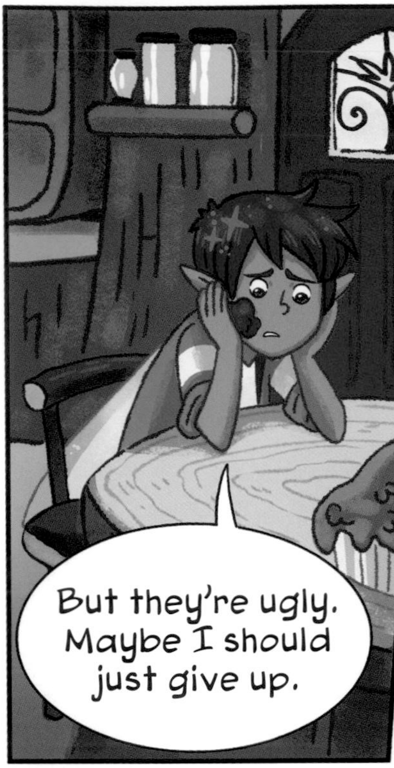
But they're ugly. Maybe I should just give up.

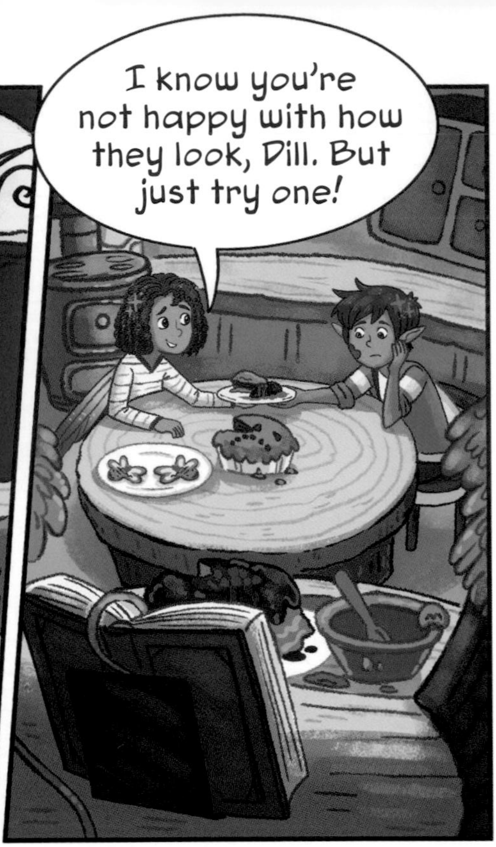
I know you're not happy with how they look, Dill. But just try one!

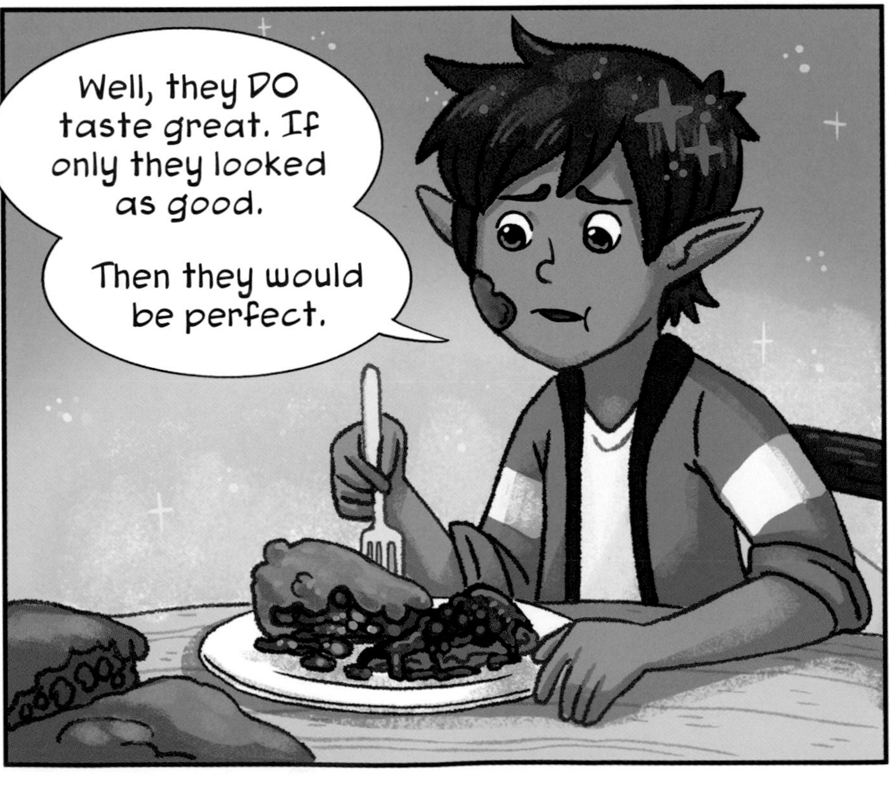
Well, they DO taste great. If only they looked as good.
Then they would be perfect.

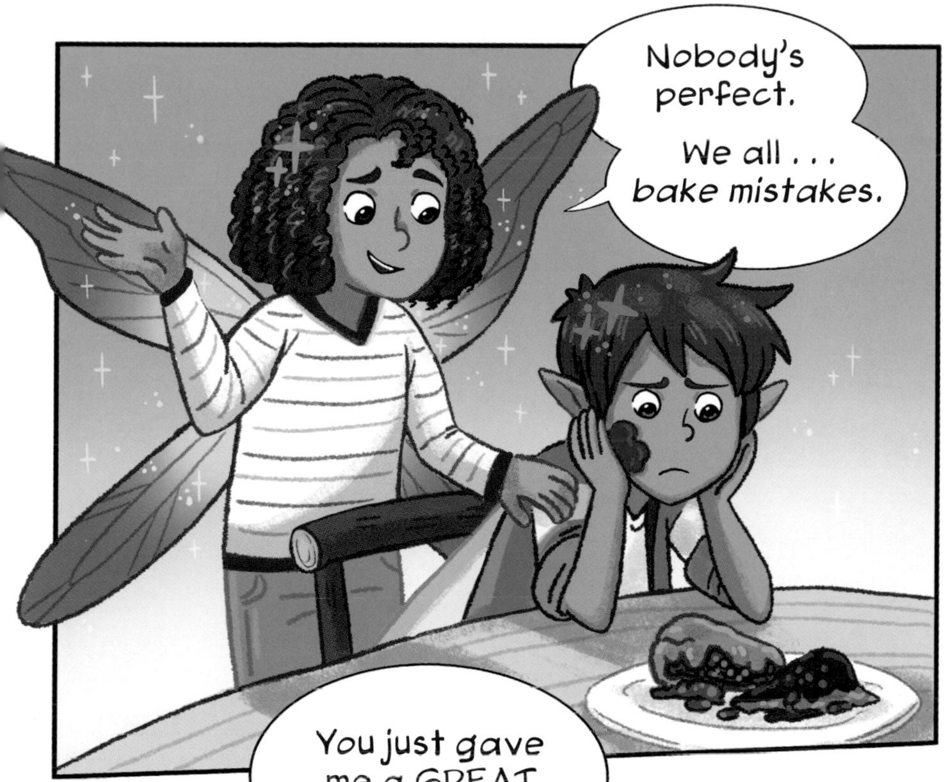
Nobody's perfect.
We all . . . bake mistakes.

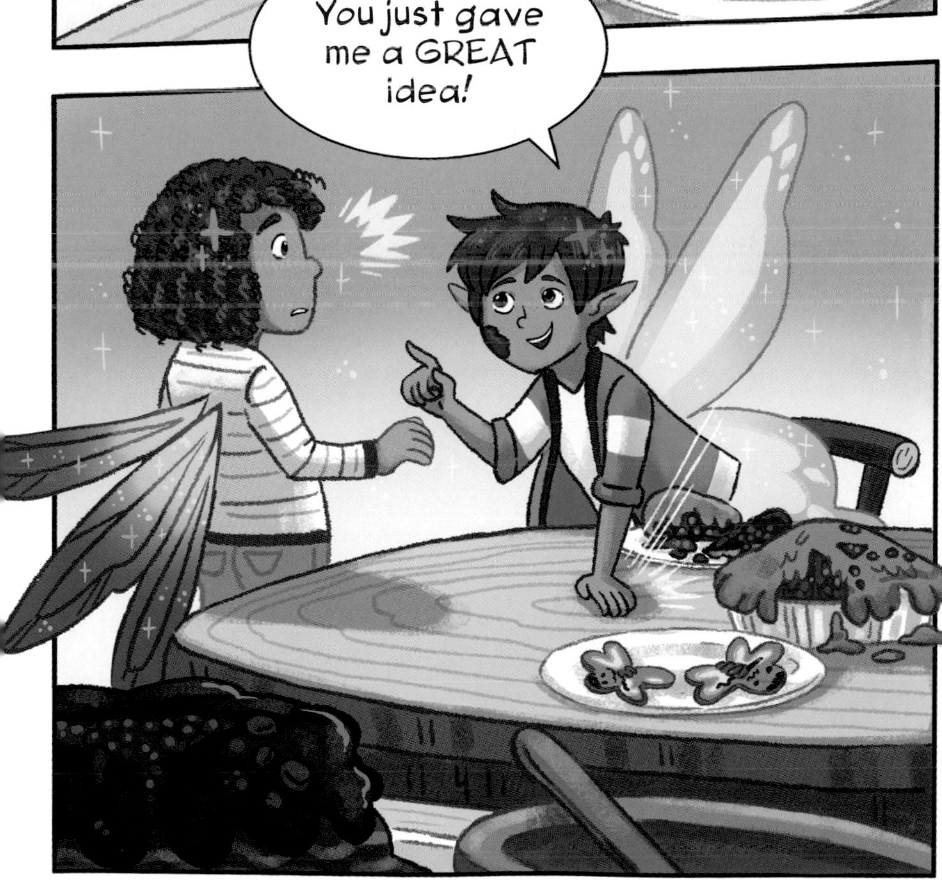
You just gave me a GREAT idea!

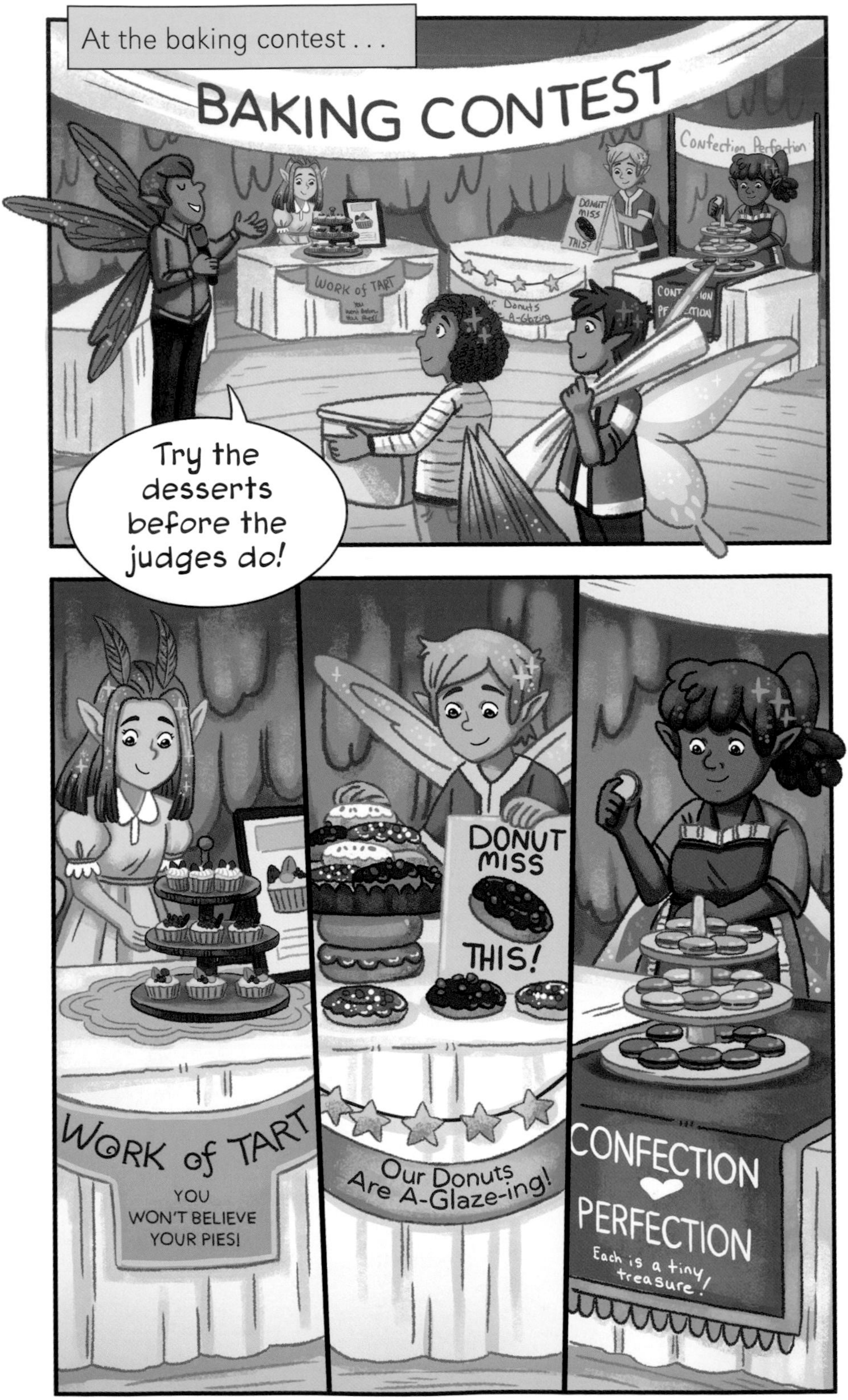
At the baking contest . . .
BAKING CONTEST
Try the desserts before the judges do!
WORK of TART
YOU WON'T BELIEVE YOUR PIES!
DONUT MISS THIS!
Our Donuts Are A-Glaze-ing!
CONFECTION PERFECTION
Each is a tiny treasure!

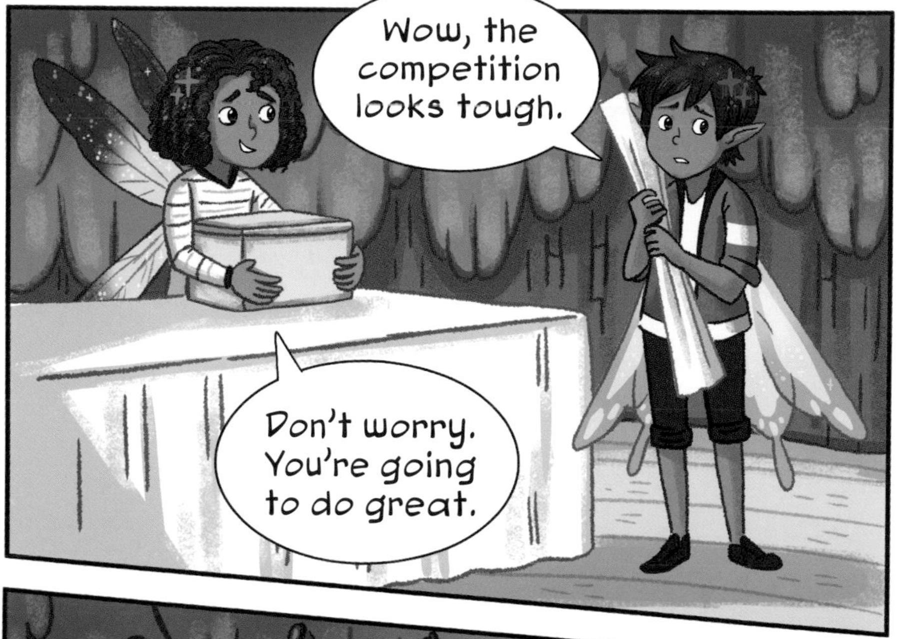
Wow, the competition looks tough.
Don't worry. You're going to do great.

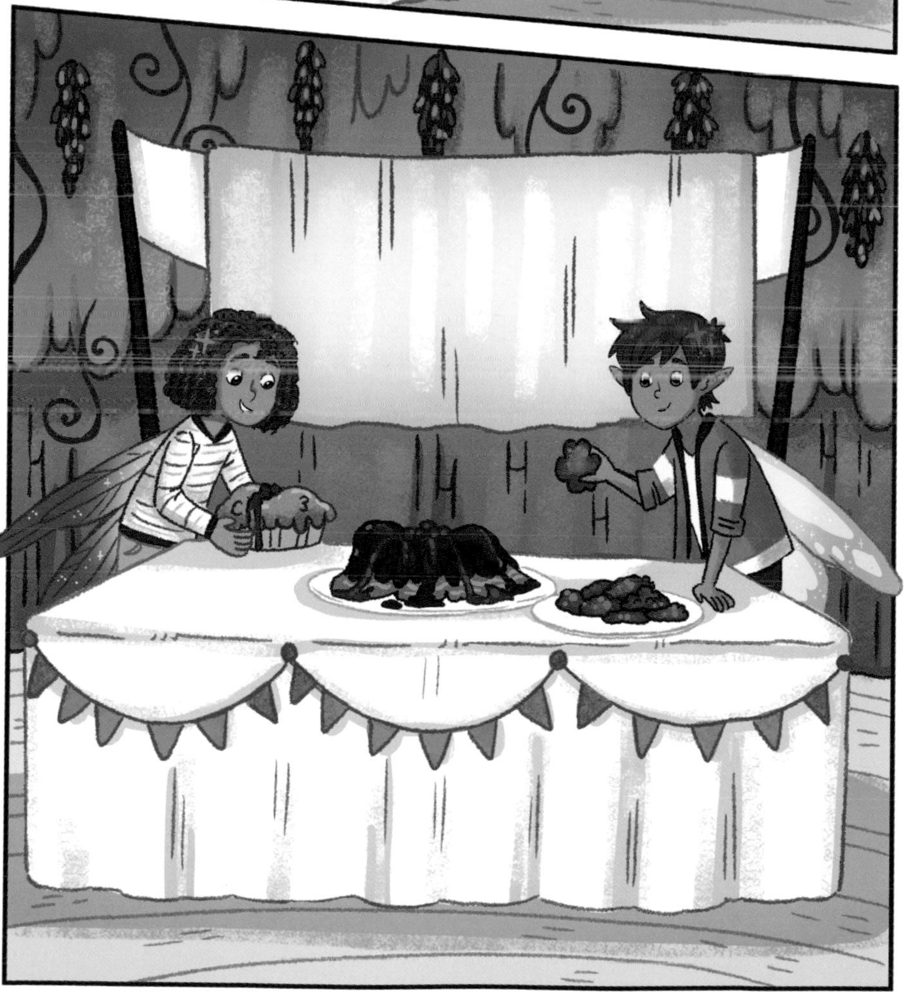

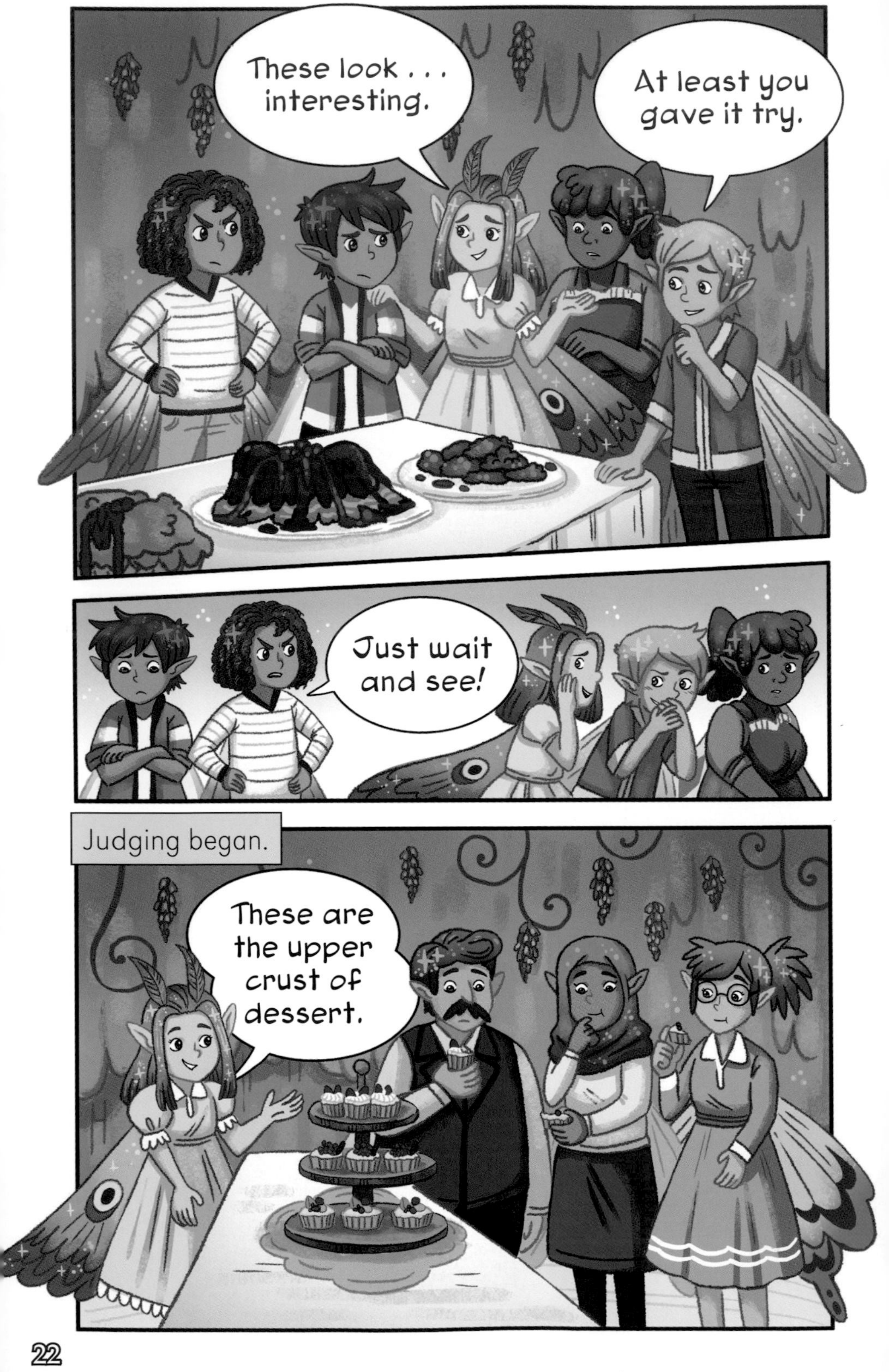
These look . . . interesting.
At least you gave it try.
Just wait and see!
Judging began.
These are the upper crust of dessert.

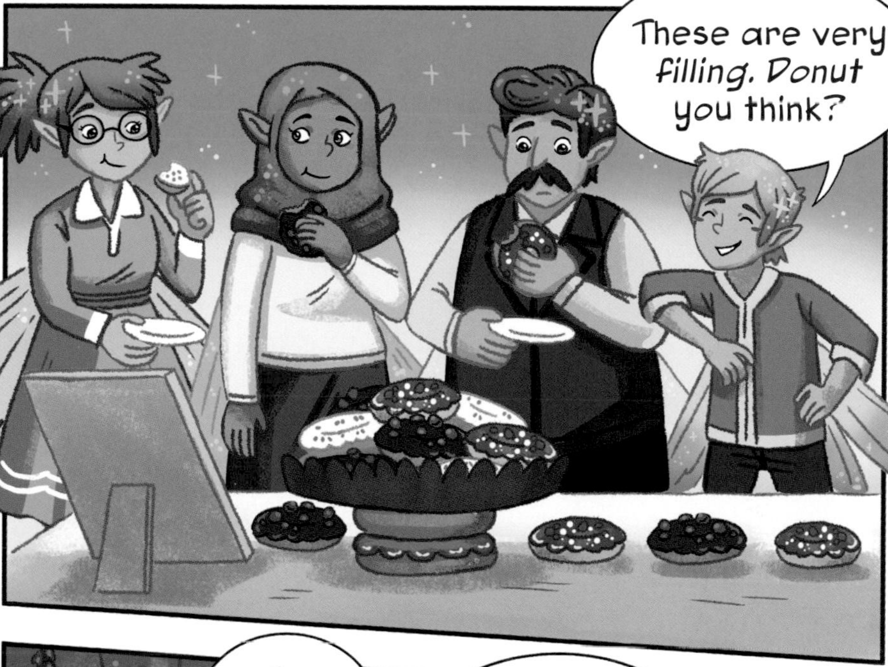
These are very filling. Donut you think?

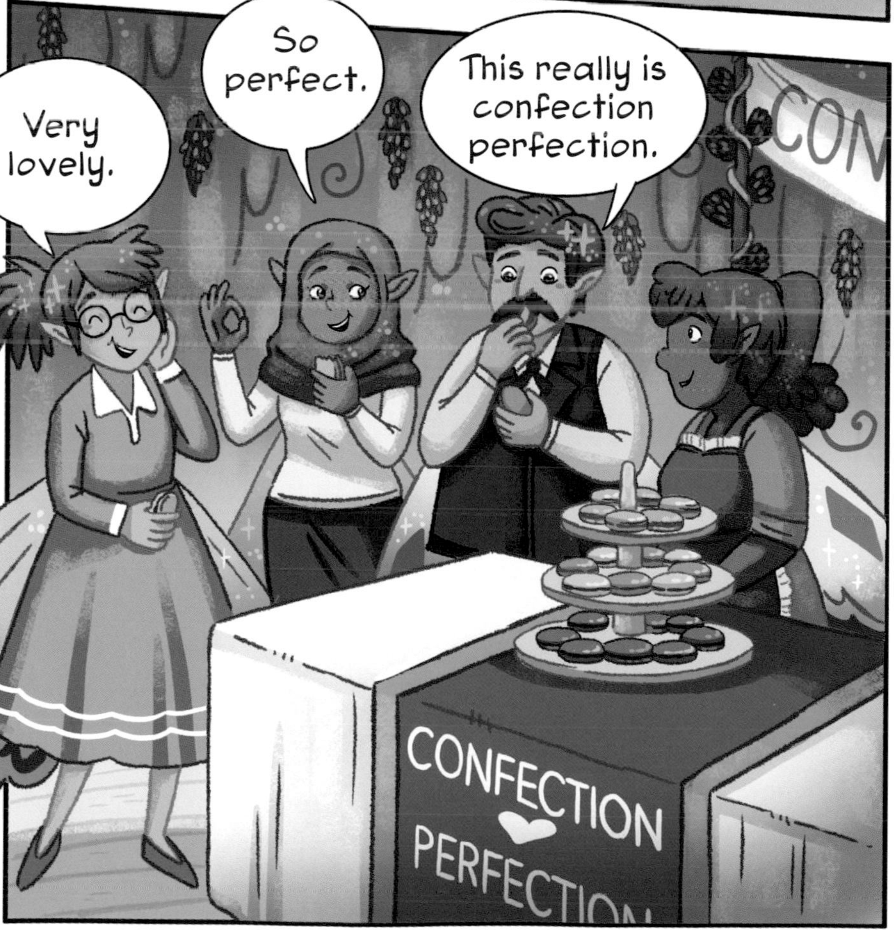
Very lovely.
So perfect.
This really is confection perfection.
CON
CONFECTION
PERFECTION

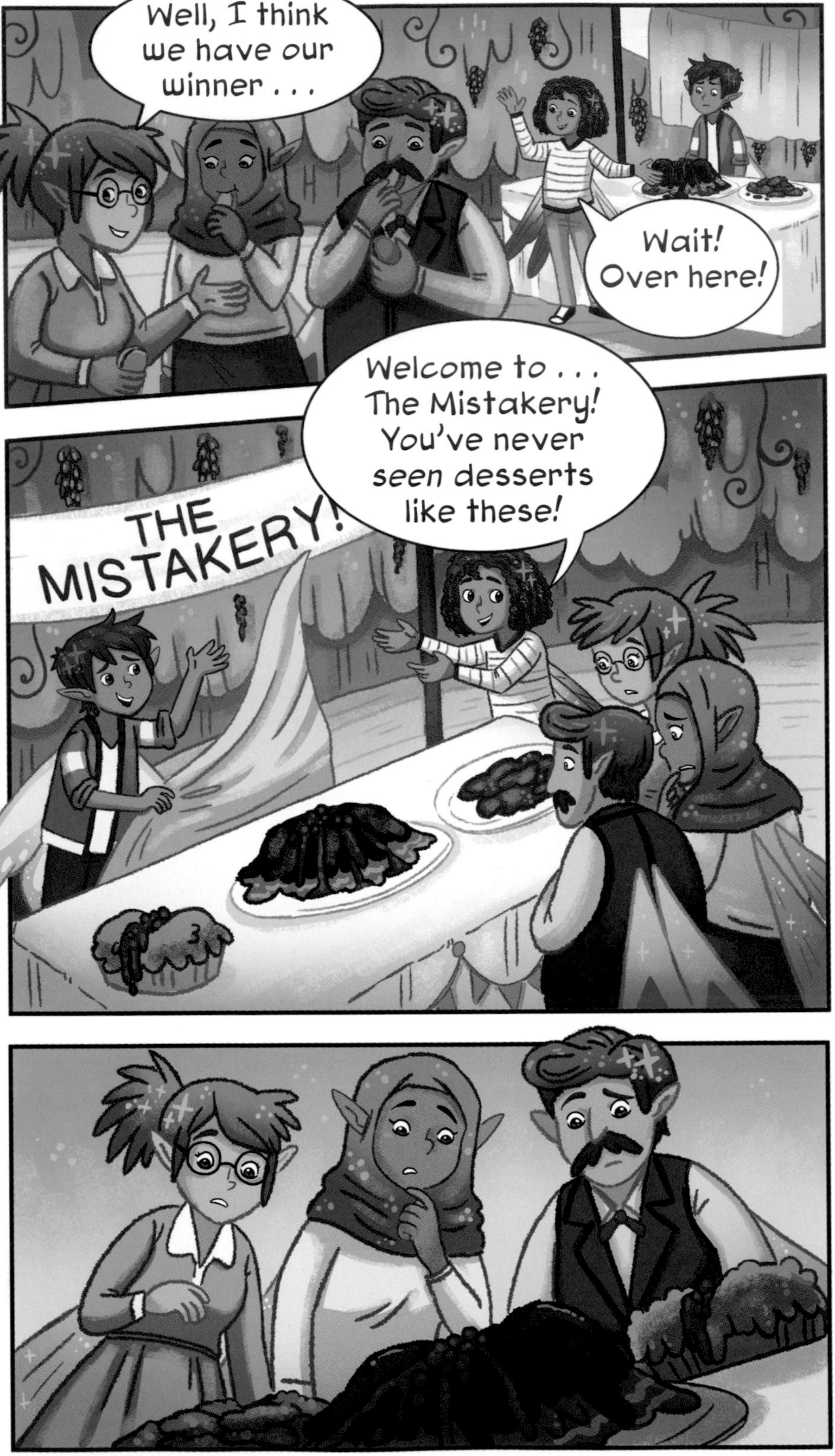

Well, I think we have our winner . . .
Wait! Over here!
Welcome to . . . The Mistakery! You've never seen desserts like these!
THE MISTAKERY!

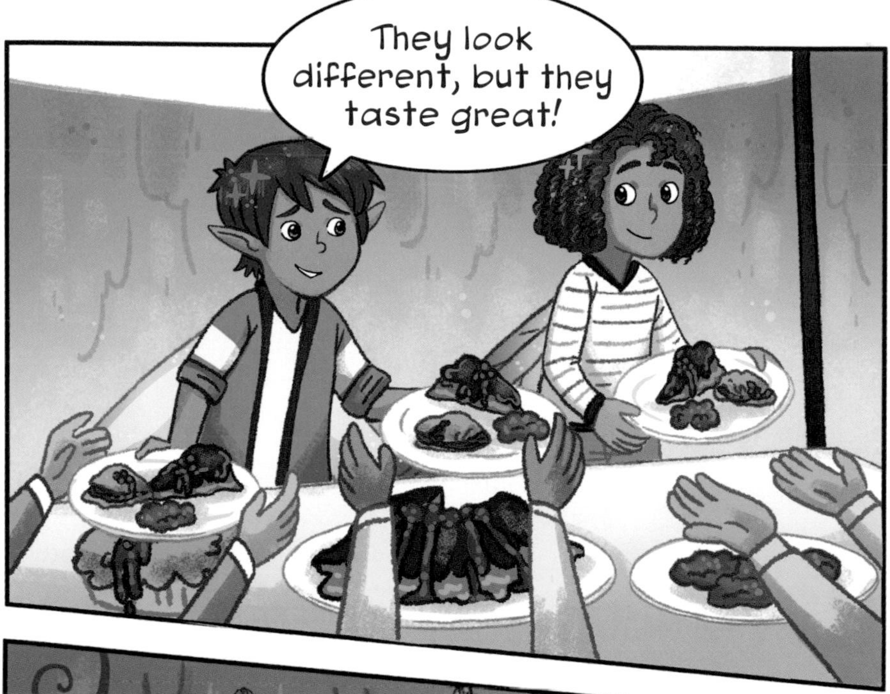
They look different, but they taste great!

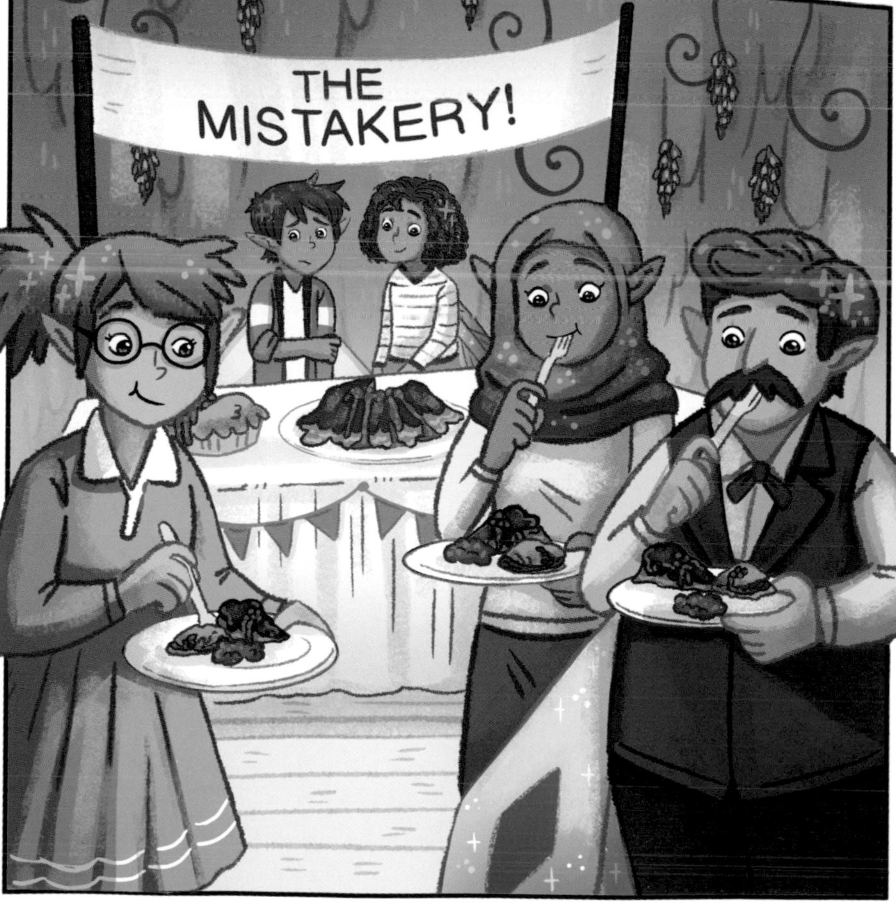
THE MISTAKERY!

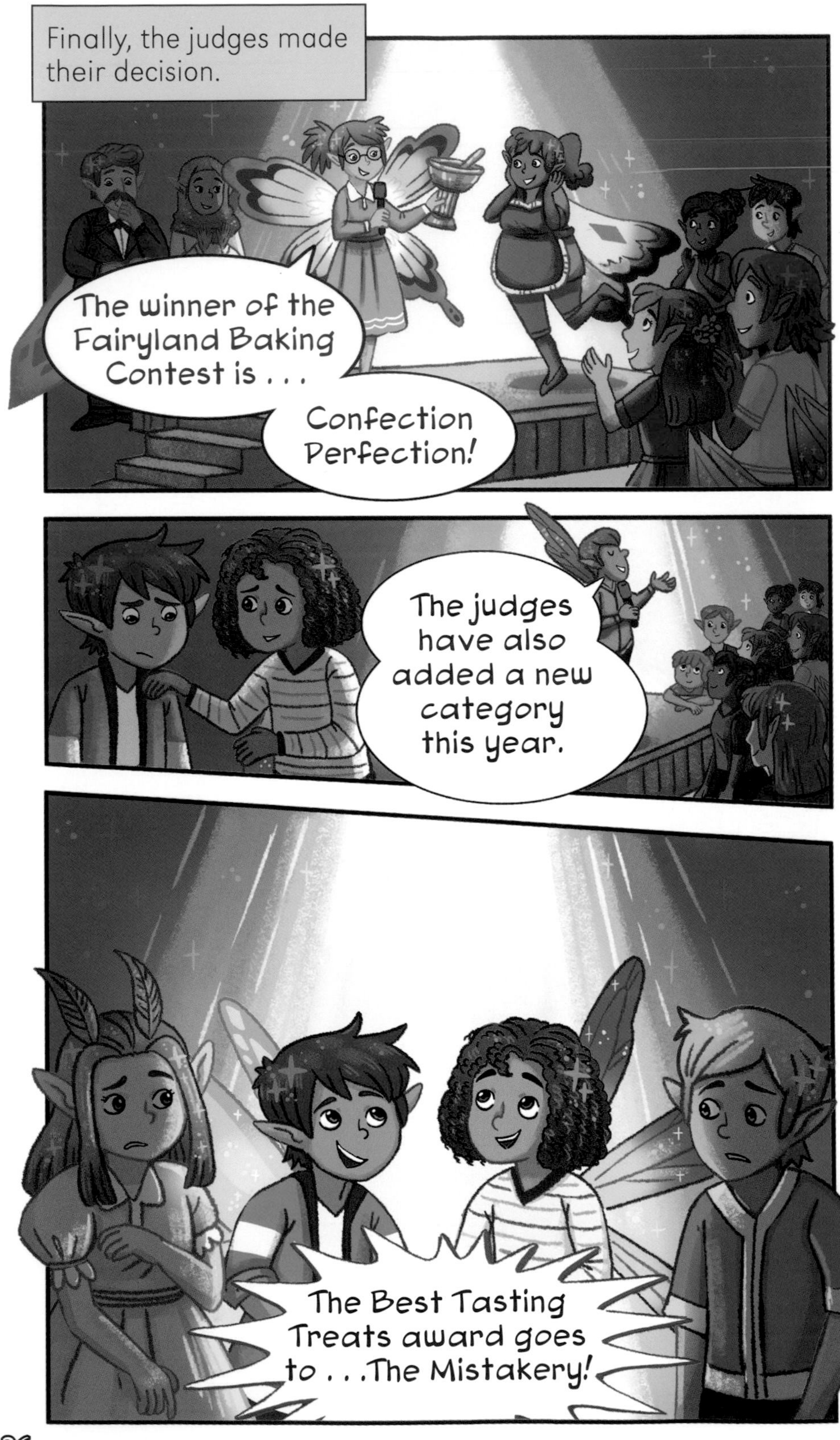
Finally, the judges made their decision.
The winner of the Fairyland Baking Contest is . . .
Confection Perfection!
The judges have also added a new category this year.
The Best Tasting Treats award goes to . . .The Mistakery!

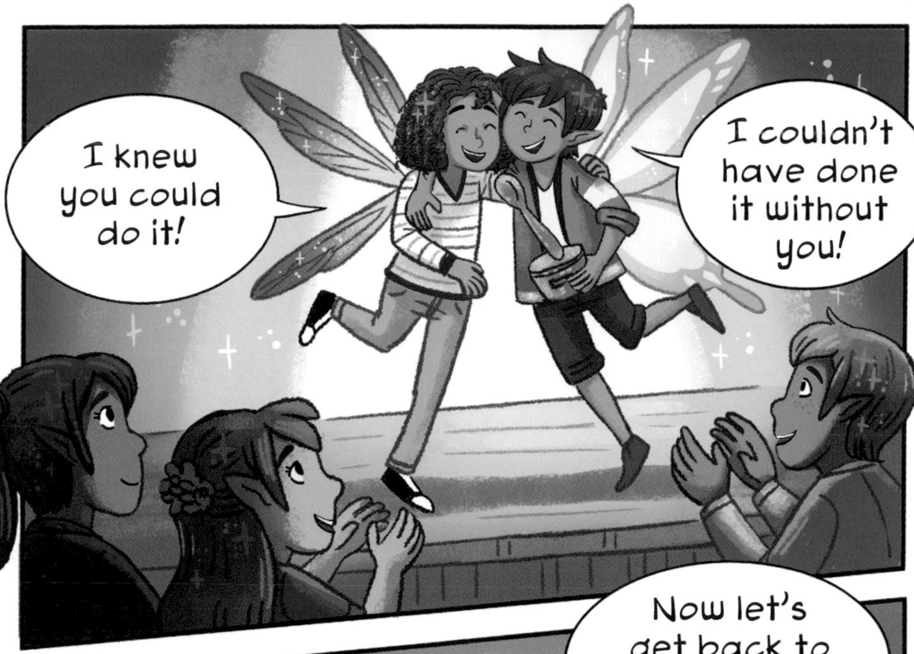
I knew you could do it!
I couldn't have done it without you!

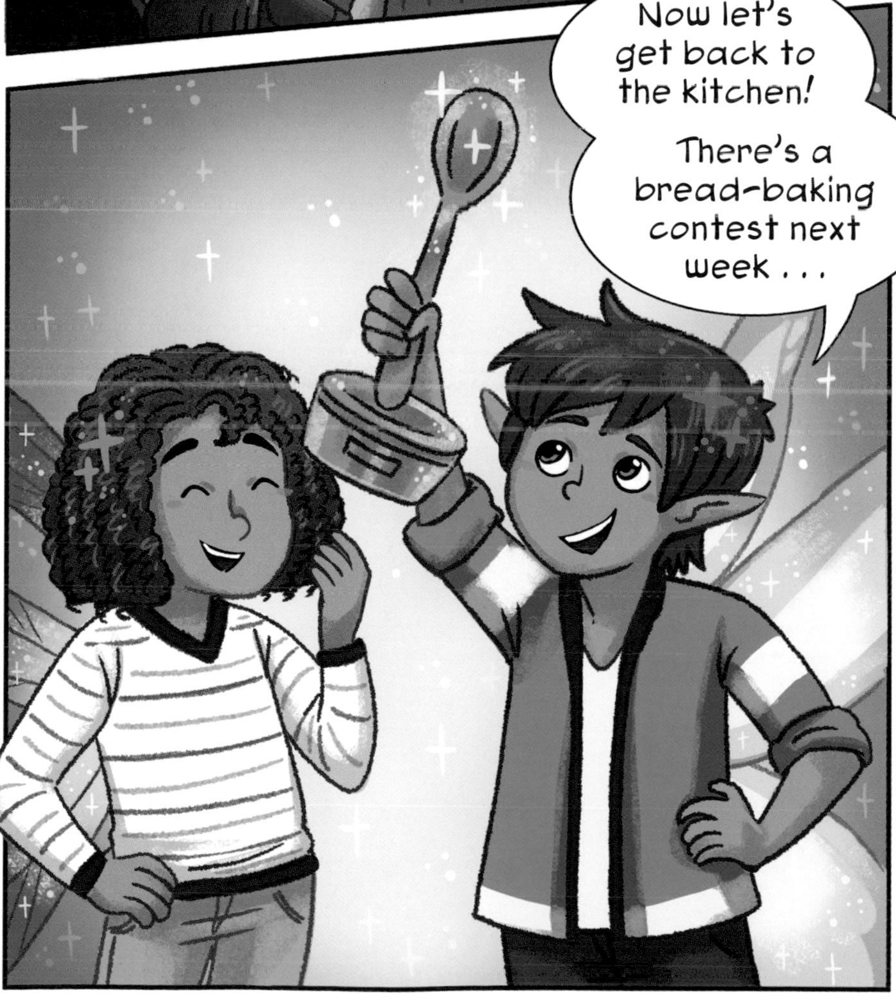
Now let's get back to the kitchen!
There's a bread-baking contest next week . . .

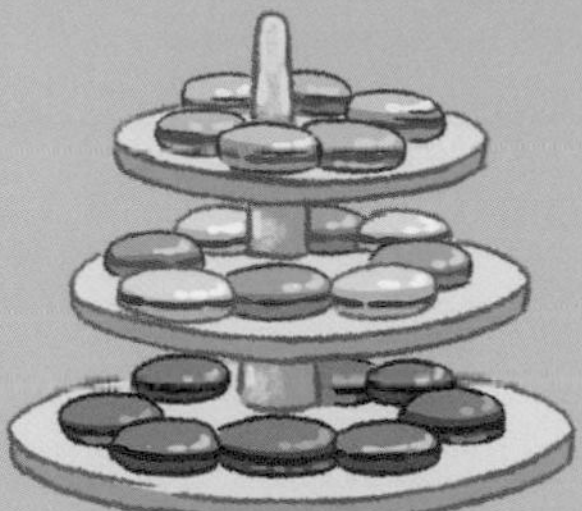

WRITING PROMPTS

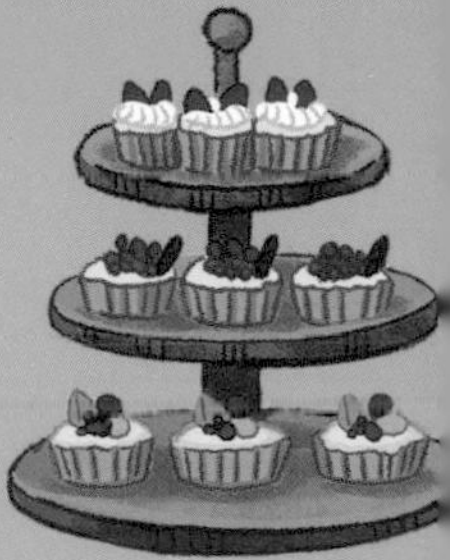

1. Try writing a recipe for a food you like. It's okay if you don't know all the ingredients! Do your best. Then draw a picture of the food when it's done.

2. Imagine you are one of the judges. Write a description of one of Dill's dishes. Make it as detailed as you can.

3. Make a poster advertising Dill's treats.

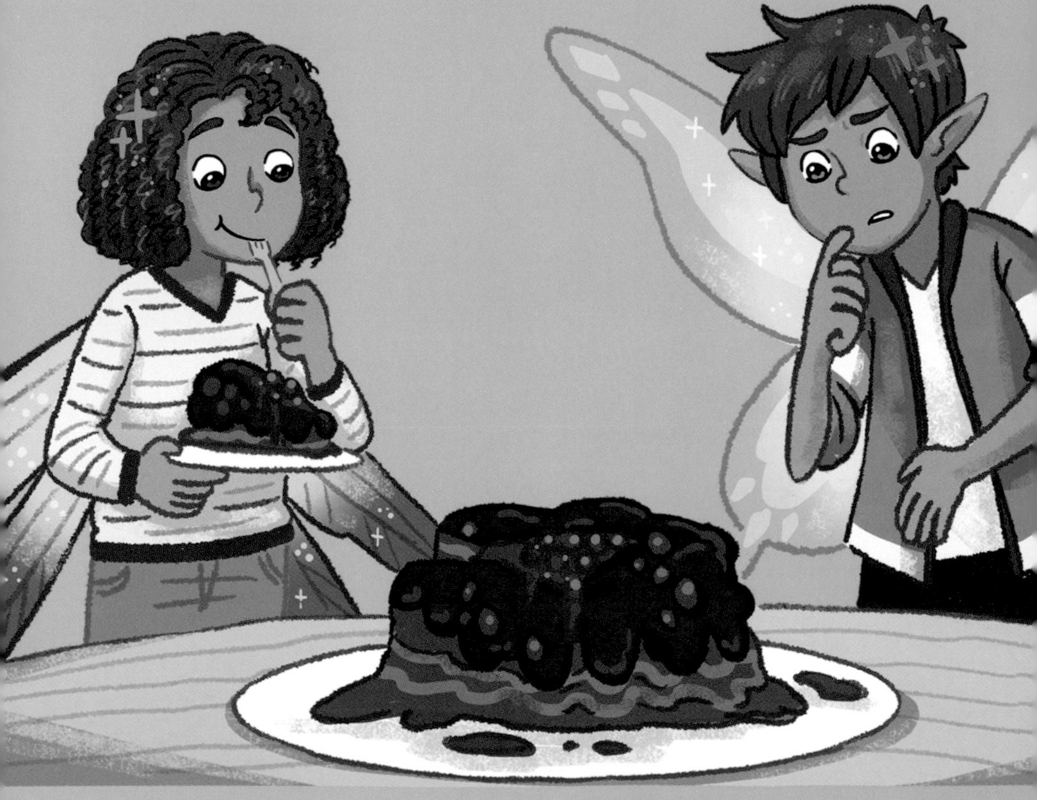

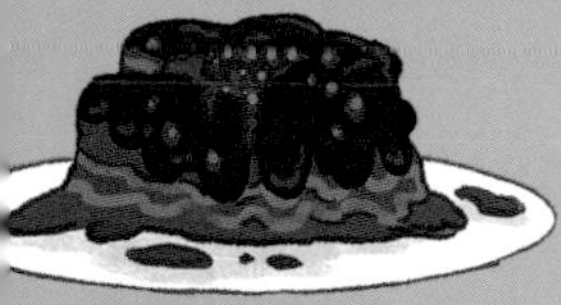

DISCUSSION QUESTIONS

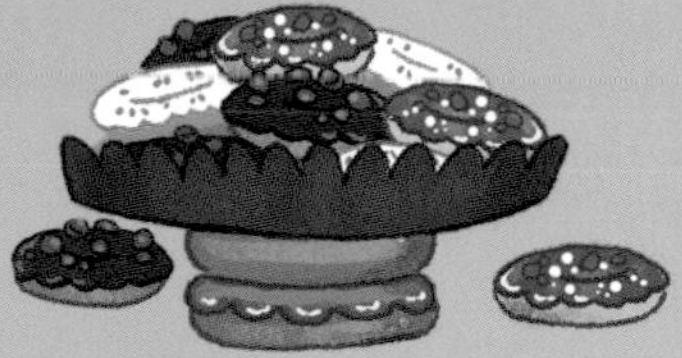

1. Have you ever tried a food that looked unusual but tasted great? What was it? Describe it to a partner.

2. Have you ever made a mistake that turned out to be a success?

3. When did you help a friend fix a mistake that they made?

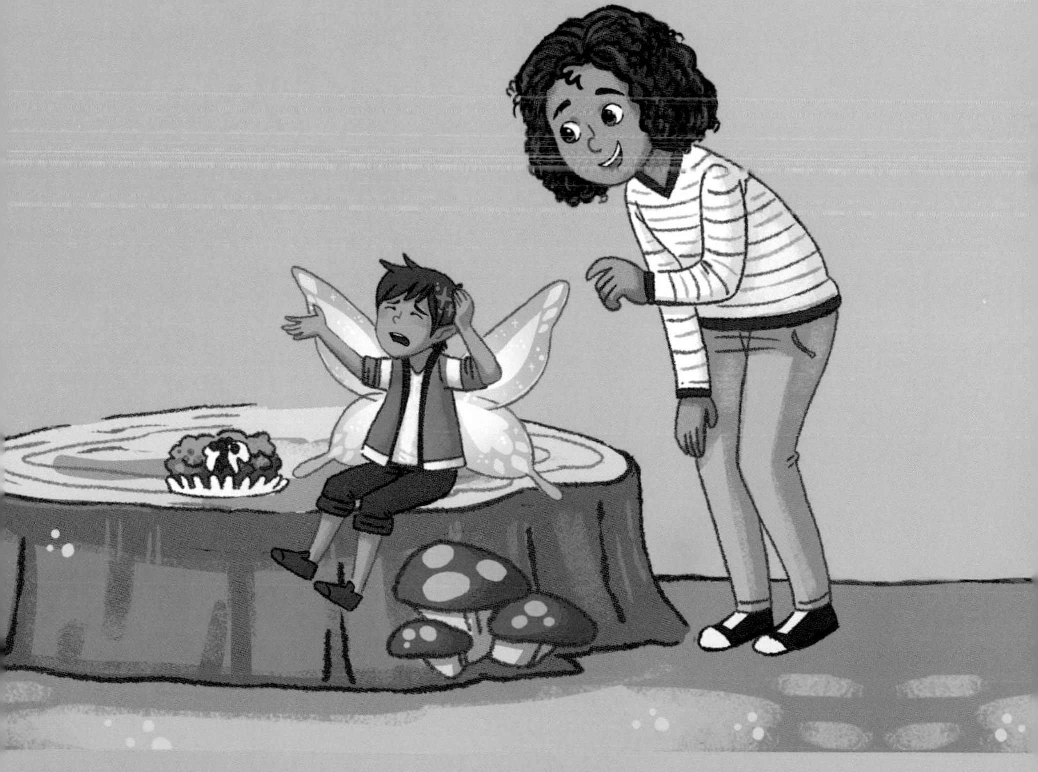

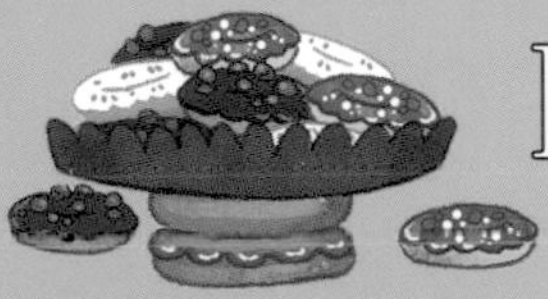

FAIRY PUFF COOKIES

Make your own journey to Fairyland with some Fairy Puff Cookies. These cookies both look *and* taste good.

Ingredients:

- 1 cup (200 grams) granulated sugar
- 1 cup (120 g) powdered sugar
- 8 eggs, room temperature
- ¼ teaspoon (4 g) cream of tartar
- ¼ teaspoon (4 g) salt
- 1 teaspoon (5 milliliters) vanilla or almond extract

Tools:

- small bowl
- medium-sized bowl
- electric mixer
- zip-top bag
- scissors
- baking sheets lined with aluminum foil

What You Do:

Step 1: Ask an adult to preheat the oven to 250°F (120°C).

Step 2: Mix the granulated sugar and powdered sugar together in the small bowl.

Step 3: Ask an adult to help separate the yolks from the egg whites. Do not get any yolk in with the whites! Put the egg whites in the medium-sized bowl. Discard the yolks.

Step 4: With an adult's help, use an electric mixer to beat the egg whites until they are foamy. Add the cream of tartar and salt, and then mix until combined.

Step 5: Add the sugar a little at a time as you continue to beat the egg whites.

Step 6: Add vanilla or almond extract. Keep beating until the egg whites are stiff and shiny. This could take as long as 10 minutes.

Step 7: Scoop the mixture into the zip-top bag. Snip off one corner of the bag. Then pipe fairy puff shapes out onto the foil-lined baking sheets.

Step 8: Bake for 1 hour until the cookies are cream-colored. Then turn the oven off. Leave the cookies inside the oven overnight, without opening the door. Then eat and enjoy!

R[redacted]AD ALL THE AMAZING DISCOVER GRAPHICS BOOKS!

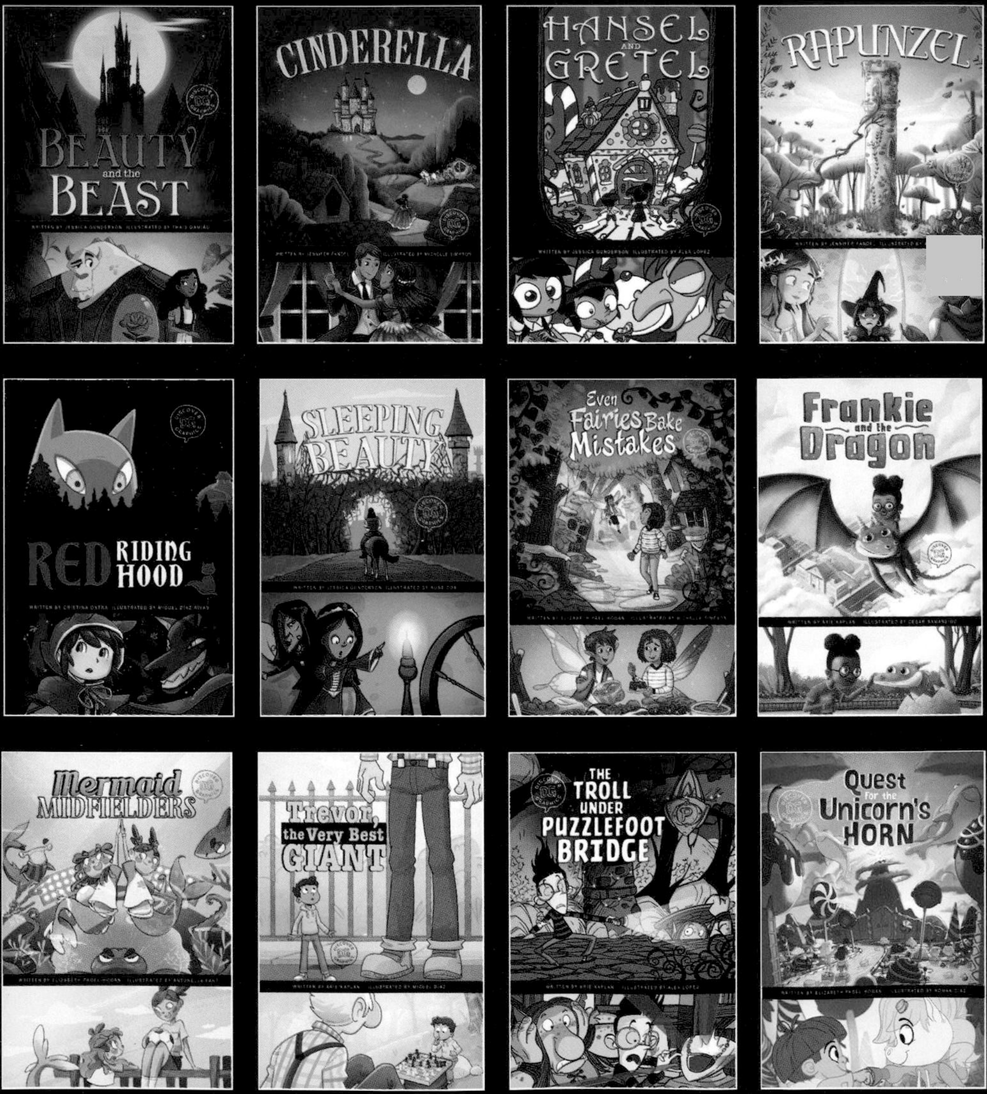
BEAUTY and the BEAST
CINDERELLA
HANSEL AND GRETEL
RAPUNZEL
RED RIDING HOOD
SLEEPING BEAUTY
Even Fairies Bake Mistakes
Frankie and the Dragon
Mermaid MIDFIELDERS
Trevor, the Very Best GIANT
THE TROLL UNDER PUZZLEFOOT BRIDGE
Quest for the Unicorn's HORN

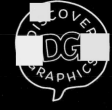